CHARMING HIM

A Met His Match Novel

LOUISA MASTERS

Charming Him

Escape to a world of glamor and excitement...

Hardworking Australian nurse Ben Adams inherits a substantial sum and decides to tour Europe. In Monaco, the home of glamour and the idle rich, he meets French billionaire playboy Léo Artois.

After getting off on the wrong foot—as happens when one accuses a stranger of being part of the Albanian mafia —their attraction blazes.

Léo, born to the top tier of society, has never known limits, and Ben, used to budgeting every cent, finds it difficult to adjust to not only Léo's world, but also the changes wealth brings to his own life.

As they make allowances for each other's foibles, Ben gradually appreciates the finer things, and Léo widens his perspective.

They both know one thing: this is not a typical holiday romance, and they're not ready to say goodbye.

To authors of category romance everywhere—thank you.

Chapter One

Ben gazed out over the Place du Casino in Monte Carlo from his table on the terrace at the Café de Paris. Even seeing it right before his eyes, with the taste of gourmet ice cream in his mouth and the promise of a heart-attack-inducing bill to come, he still couldn't quite believe he was there. But then, it had been like that in every place he'd visited so far. His European Odyssey, as his BFF called it, was like a living dream, despite having been in progress for nearly three months already. He'd made his way through the UK and Ireland, France, Spain, and Portugal. Italy was next, but first he was taking a precious week to just loll around in the land of the idle rich.

Monaco.

It had always seemed a symbol of the ultimate luxury to Ben. Even before he'd gone to work for Mrs. K., he'd lingered over tales of the glamorous principality, although he'd never planned to visit. No, his travel had always been closer to home, and when he'd dreamed of something farther afield, it was always of a more "sensible" locale than Monaco—somewhere he could combine a great deal of sightseeing with more lazy pursuits, and stick to a narrow budget.

He didn't have to concern himself with that anymore.

As the May sun sank farther and twilight descended on the city, he scraped up the last melted bits of his dessert, then licked it off the spoon with blissful slowness. Never had he imagined he would ever pay quite so much for ice cream, but wow, what ice cream! He'd actually embarrassed himself in his enjoyment of it, moaning over the first few spoonfuls in a way that had attracted attention from passersby. He hadn't quite been able to bring himself to eat an entire meal at the Café de Paris, not when the cost of one dinner would have covered his weekly food budget at home, but he was content to pay the price for dessert and people watching—hence his choice of a table right by the road. From there, he could see both the rest of the café and its diners, and the people strolling the square, visiting the casinos and the Hotel de Paris across from the café, or simply taking in the old-world grandeur and snapping photos. So far by his count, Monte Carlo was pretty evenly balanced between tourists and old men with much younger female companions. He wondered idly where the old men who wanted much younger male companions were. Not that he was interested in being a gigolo to a rich man, but it would be nice to know the opportunity existed.

He snorted, causing the couple at the next table to glance disdainfully at him—again. He wasn't exactly gigolo material. Gigolos usually gave a damn about their appearance for one thing, and Ben had given up caring how he looked in nursing school. Nowadays, he only just took the time to wash his face and make sure his always-wayward short dark hair wasn't sticking up too badly. His habit of shopping in thrift and discount stores and then wearing his clothes until they were about to fall apart probably didn't give him the perfectly put-together look he imagined gigolos aimed for, either. In fact, he really needed to replace the battered runners that were his current "casual" shoes. One was worn to the point that his toe, on the verge of popping through for weeks, had finally made an appearance, and he'd garnered quite a few askance looks over the past week. No way was he buying new shoes in any of the shops he'd seen in Monaco so far, though. It would have to wait until Italy—he could probably find a street market somewhere.

The lights came on around the square, and he finally got to see what he'd been waiting for, what Mrs. K. had spoken about with such a wistful tone and a far-off gleam in her eye. She hadn't been wrong—the facade of the "old" casino did glow warmly. As he gazed around, he noticed that while he'd been lost in thought about gigolos, there had been a subtle change in the populace of the square. He could still pick the "tourists" like him, but even they were more dressed up and had put their cameras away. More, now, were those who wanted to see and be seen, and those who considered the city their personal playground. Even his untutored eye could spot the expensive designer clothes and real jewels—not to mention the high-end vehicles, keys casually tossed to the casino valets as their owners strolled inside.

A group of men in front of the Hotel de Paris caught his eye, and his breath stopped in his chest. They walked— no, strode—boldly toward the casino, their arrogance almost a palpable thing. People moved out of their way, whether consciously or not. All five were big men, all dressed in dark trousers and blazers, all but one dark-haired and dark-skinned, but one man stood head and shoulders above—

Well, no, he doesn't. Ben chided himself for being fanciful. The man in question was actually not the tallest in the group; two others were slightly taller. They all had to be at least six feet, though, which made them giants beside his own five foot eight, even if they hadn't also been well-built. But the not-tallest one… his height didn't matter. If he'd been five feet, he still would have walked the same way, as though he owned the square, the principality, and possibly part of France too.

And all the people who lived there were his slaves, existing purely to serve his pleasure.

Stop. Ben shook his head. He wasn't usually so imaginative. Still, he couldn't help but stare as the group came to a stop at the steps of the casino. Just the way the man moved made Ben's dick beg for attention. He hadn't had a reaction like that to a fully dressed stranger since he was a teenager. Something about the not-tallest man made Ben want to throw himself at him and plead shamelessly to be fucked.

Which was stupid. He'd rarely ever had sex with hot strangers. Or any strangers, for that matter.

One of the men opened a satchel Ben hadn't noticed and handed something—a wallet?—to *him*, the not-tallest man, who put it in his inside breast pocket. What a dick. Couldn't even carry his own wallet. Ben had run into a lot of men like that during his trip, what with staying at the best hotels for once, and they'd all looked at him as though he was something unpleasant they'd stepped in, even though none of them seemed to do anything productive with their lives.

The man with the satchel and the blond one turned and walked back toward the hotel while the other three went up the steps to the casino. The doormen scrambled to get the doors, and even from such a distance, Ben saw the way they greeted the not-tallest man, the deference they showed.

His imagination went wild.

Who was this man with such commanding presence? Why didn't he carry his own wallet? Was he so rich and spoiled that carrying his own belongings was beneath him? Nobility, perhaps, or even royalty? This was Europe after all. Or maybe he was part of a criminal organization, and the satchel guy was his lackey? Ben had heard a lot lately about the activities of the Albanian mafia, and this guy's coloring fit.

More important than anything else… what did he actually look like? From where Ben sat, with distance and the shadows of night hindering him, he'd been unable to make out the man clearly. But someone with so much raw sex appeal in just his bearing had to be attractive… right? There had to be some reason people were so deferential on sight, why he so clearly expected that treatment. Why Ben's hormones wanted him to smear honey all over him and lick it off.

Slowly.

He had to find out.

Galvanized into action, he flagged down his waitress—who looked affronted by his urgency and unsubtle gestures—and paid his bill before striding toward the casino. Well… trying to stride. In reality, he nearly walked into one of the bollards protecting the valet parking spaces, and then staggered awkwardly in an attempt to regain his balance. There were titters, but when he finally was able to look up, nobody seemed to be paying him any attention. Face flaming, he marched determinedly onward. He had to see the not-tallest man up close. Had to get a better idea of who he could be, why people scrambled to let him pass.

The first real hurdle came at the entrance to the casino.

Rather than open the door, the doormen cast disparaging gazes over him.

He reached for the door handle. After all, he was a grown man, right? He could open a door by himself.

One of the uniformed doormen sidled sideways, blocking him. Ben blinked, but before he could say anything, the man spoke.

In French.

Ben winced. He'd taken Italian in school, and that had firmly established that languages were something he'd never be good at. His knowledge of French was limited to *bonjour*, *s'il vous plaît*, *merci*, *anglais*, and *croissant*. He'd been relying heavily on gestures, big smiles, and his phrase book…, which he'd left at his hotel because he'd been assured that everyone spoke English in Monaco.

"Ah… do you speak *anglais*?" he tried, pairing the words with his biggest smile. The doormen exchanged glances, and it seemed the look for *this guy is a total dumbarse* transcended language. One of them opened the door a tiny bit and slipped inside. Ben stood staring at the other one, who was still blocking his way. The casino was open to the public; he knew it was. There was a small fee to go into the gaming rooms, but it was free to stand in the foyer and gawk at the architecture, so he shouldn't have to pay at the door. He had the right to go into the casino, damn it, just like all the rich bastards he'd watched enter already.

Crap, he needed a translator.

Maybe he could use Google Translate? Even if he couldn't pronounce the words, he could let the other man read them off the screen. He was fumbling in his pocket for his phone when the door opened again—wider this time—and the other doorman came back out, accompanied by a man in a black suit.

"Good evening," the man said with a French accent, smiling politely.

"You speak English," Ben exclaimed in relief. "That's so good, because I was about to try using Google Translate, and I'm pretty sure nothing good was going to come of it."

The man's smile wavered slightly, and Ben immediately felt like a dork. What was wrong with his stupid brain-mouth filter?

He drew himself up... and was still two inches shorter than Suit Man.

"I wish to enter the casino," he declared, then tried to hide a wince at how pompous he sounded.

The man nodded. "Yes, and we would love to have you as our guest. But you see, we have a dress code at the Casino de Monte-Carlo. Shorts and trainers are strictly forbidden."

Ben blinked. Had they lost something in translation? *Trainers? Like, personal trainers? Why would they forbid—* Something he'd heard in England clicked in his brain. "Oh, you mean runners." He looked down at himself. Yep, he was wearing both shorts *and* runners, thereby well and truly violating the dress code.

Well, crap.

He could go back to his hotel and change. Total walking time would be barely five minutes, less if not for that damn hill. But it seemed silly to go back to his hotel to change clothes, then come back to the casino... just so he could look at a man he didn't know. This whole thing was kind of silly, really. He was a levelheaded guy, sensible—he was a nurse, for God's sake. His last boyfriend had accused him of having no imagination, no creativity whatsoever. Why did he care that some random probably hot guy acted like a god deigning to mingle with mere mortals?

"Perhaps sir would like to visit the Casino Café de Paris?" Suit Man said smoothly. "There is no dress code there. I'm sure you would be more comfortable." Although his words were perfectly polite, there was just a hint of disdain in his gaze that made Ben's mind up.

Silly was the way to go.

Chapter Two

Léonard Khalid Artois looked up from the roulette wheel when his cousin elbowed him.

"What?" he asked, not really as annoyed as he made his voice sound. Roulette was not his thing.

"Your little bunny is here," Malik said, nodding toward the door. Léo turned immediately. Sure enough, there was the man from Café de Paris, craning his neck awkwardly as he looked around the Salle Blanche, a slightly stunned expression on his plain face. He'd changed clothes, but the long trousers and collared shirt did nothing to disguise his thin, almost gangly frame, and his short hair still stuck out in all directions. While not unpleasant to look at, he wasn't at all eye-catching—and yet, while waiting for Karim outside the Hotel de Paris, Léo hadn't been able to take his eyes off the man, or the way he licked his spoon with utter bliss on his face. Hence Malik dubbing him "bunny"— apparently Léo had looked at him as though he were prey.

Léo cast a quick glance at Karim. His young cousin was visiting Monaco as part of the coming-of-age European tour his father, Léo's uncle, had gifted him. He'd been there for three days, and Léo was glad he was leaving tomorrow. The boy was absolutely exhausting, and insisted on "experiencing everything," which was why they were staying at the Hotel de Paris even though Léo and Malik both lived in Monaco. Now Karim was enthralled by the roulette wheel, despite Malik having explained to him how slim the odds of winning were.

"I'll watch him," Malik said, correctly interpreting Léo's concern. "Give me his wallet, and you go get your bunny. I'll make sure Karim gets back to the hotel… and tell him you say goodbye, if you don't make it back before he leaves."

Léo fished Karim's wallet from his pocket and handed it to Malik with a quelling look. He hadn't absolutely decided to fuck the little bun—the man. He was just going to say hello, flirt a little, and see how things went.

Across the room, his quarry was wandering around with a lost look, seemingly searching for something but showing little interest in the tables. He narrowly avoided collision with a shipping magnate and his wife, and Léo winced.

It took him only a few moments to cross the room, nodding to acquaintances as he went, and come up behind the stranger.

"Bonsoir," he said, laying a hand on the man's shoulder. He started and whirled around, losing his balance and almost falling. Léo grabbed his arm and hauled him upright before he could knock anyone over. "Excusez-moi, je ne—"

"I don't speak French," the man interrupted, a desperate edge to his voice as he regained his balance. He looked up, and his eyes went wide as he took Léo in. "S-sorry. Um—"

"Then it is just as well that I speak English," Léo said

smoothly. He hadn't quite placed the man's accent—definitely not American, and not really British, either. South African, maybe, or Australian. Still gripping his arm, Léo steered them out of the flow of traffic and toward the bar. A quick, steely glance at a couple there resulted in two empty stools, and he settled his bunny on one of them while the bartender scuttled over to take their order.

"What will you drink?" he asked the man, who was muttering vague protests about not needing to sit. Brown eyes blinked at him.

"Um… I don't really drink much. Jack and Coke?"

Amusement and annoyance warred in Léo, and he turned to the bartender. "Champagne," he ordered, not bothering to specify. They knew his tastes here, and if they didn't, they'd find out before daring to bring anything. The man smiled and nodded and hurried away.

"I don't speak French, but even I know that champagne doesn't mean Jack and Coke." There was an edge to Bunny's voice, and when Léo looked at him, a mutinous set to his mouth.

"You cannot come to the Casino de Monte-Carlo in Monaco and drink cheap blended whiskey mixed with sugar and chemicals," he instructed.

"Pretty sure I can," the man muttered, and Léo smothered a smile, sure it would not be appreciated.

"But you should not. You are far from home, and have the opportunity for a new experience in a glamorous"—he gestured to their surroundings, knowing that for many tourists the mosaic bar and terrace of the Salle Blanche, combined with the elaborate architecture and decor, were the height of sophistication—"place, a place of legend. The Casino de Monte-Carlo! Now is your chance to try something you never would in your ordinary life," he finished, taking in the lower-quality off-the-rack clothing and laying things on a little thick. The shell-shocked look was fading, replaced by a faintly suspicious one.

"Are you a con man?"

Insult flared. "Why would you ask such a thing?" Léo demanded. What was wrong with the man?

"That's not an answer." Bunny started to get up. "I've heard all about men who prey on tourists, and I'm not—"

"Oh, sit down." Léo nudged the man back onto the stool. "I'm not a con man. My name is Léo Artois, and anyone here can vouch for me." He pulled his wallet from his hip pocket. "Look, here's my identification." If anything, that made the bunny—he really needed to learn the man's name—more suspicious.

"That's not where your wallet was before."

For the first time in a long while, Léo was speechless. Was Bunny stalking him? And what was he talking about? "Quelle?"

"I don't speak French," Bunny reminded him.

Léo recovered somewhat as the bartender delivered two chilled flutes and an ice bucket containing a bottle of Krug Clos du Mesnil. He was fairly certain it wasn't his preferred 1998 vintage, but both the 2000 and 2003 were acceptable. In short order, the bartender opened the bottle and poured. As the man left them, Léo lifted the flutes and offered one to the bunny.

"I don't really like champagne," the man said, eying the glass dubiously. "But I guess you're right. How often will I get the chance to drink champers in Monte Carlo?" He took the glass and sipped cautiously. His eyes went wide. "*That* is not champagne."

Amused again, almost against his will, Léo took a sip himself. The 2000. "It most certainly is," he said, allowing himself to smile as Bunny took another, longer swallow, then fumbled to remove the cloth from the bottle. "What are you doing?"

"I want to see the label. Maybe I can get this at home." He uncovered the bottle and then drew his phone from his pocket. Léo stopped him before he could snap a picture.

"No photos are permitted in here," he advised quietly. Rules did not normally apply to him, but he was in favor of anything that protected his privacy.

Bunny looked abashed. "Oh. I didn't think. I'll just make a note then." He fiddled with the phone for a few moments, then gasped, his head snapping up. "Do you know how much this stuff costs?" He set his glass down carefully on the bar, as if merely holding it would incur a fee. Léo winced.

"One must pay for quality, but never speak of price."

"Well, you should!" the man insisted hotly. "Most people have monthly mortgage payments that cost less than this bottle."

Irritation took over as Léo's last traces of amusement fled. "The bottle is open and thus paid for now. Will you waste it, or will you enjoy it as it is meant to be?"

Bunny's face flooded with color. "I beg your pardon. I didn't mean to be rude." He looked longingly at his flute, still sitting on the bar, then back at Léo. "Are you sure you're not a con man?"

"Absolument."

"That means yes, right?"

Léo couldn't stop the smile. "Absolutely."

The man took a deep breath and stuck out his hand. "Ben Adams." Léo took the hand and shook it solemnly, then, on a whim, lifted it to his mouth and whispered a kiss across Ben's knuckles. Ben squeaked, a sound Léo found utterly endearing, and yanked his hand away, grabbed his glass, and took a gulp.

"Er, it was Léo, wasn't it?" he asked, mangling the pronunciation of Léo's name with his accent.

"Yes. Léonard Artois." Léo injected every ounce of pomposity he could into the words, channeling his father.

"That sounds like a very French name," Ben said guilelessly, taking another sip of his champagne and then looking at the glass in wonder.

"I'm very French," Léo replied, lifting his own glass to his lips. He knew the reason for Ben's comment, of course —he took after his Saudi mother's family in looks.

"So you're not a member of the Albanian mafia?" Ben asked, and then looked mortified when Léo choked on his champagne. "I'm so sorry. This is why I don't drink much."

"Why—why would you even think such a thing?" Léo asked when he'd gotten his breath back. He was caught between being mortally insulted, or utterly charmed by the crimson flush on Ben's cheeks.

"No reason, really. I was just being silly." Bunny was chewing on his lower lip now, eyes downcast, and Léo reached out, caught hold of his chin, and tipped up his face. A slight shiver ran through Ben's jaw under his hand, and sexual awareness surged in Léo's gut.

"It seems an odd thing to be silly about," he commented, and Ben cringed. "But something must have made you think it. You'd better tell me, so I can make certain no one else has the same impression."

Ben pulled his chin free. "It's really nothing. No one with an ounce of sense would think it, I swear. I just.... Look, since I've already made a total arse of myself, can you tell me why you don't carry your own wallet? And then I'll go away and you'll never have to see me again."

"That would be a shame," Léo said automatically, then realized with a great deal of surprise that he actually meant it. "But why do you keep talking about my wallet? And who else would carry it if not me? I showed you my identification—you know I have my wallet."

Bunny—Léo could not stop thinking of him thus—squared his shoulders and took another gulp of champagne, draining the glass. The bartender was there immediately to top him up, and his faint protest faded when Léo raised an eyebrow.

"I saw you outside," Ben said after yet another fortifying sip. "This stuff is so good. I think I just want to drink this for the rest of my life. It would be a short life, because paying for champagne like this would leave no money for food, clothes, or shelter, but it would be a good short life."

Amusement mixed with alarm as Léo realized his bunny was well and truly on the path to being sloshed—after less than two glasses of champagne. Although he normally had no time for men who couldn't hold their liquor—nothing was so crass as a drunk, after all—he found Ben's guileless innocence rather charming.

Perhaps Karim's company had warped his mind.

"You saw me outside," he prompted, determined to know why this naïve little tourist thought he could be part of the Albanian mafia.

"Yeah! You were outside. With your friends. And you were all like, we're so much better. And taller. Except you're not the tallest. And if a truck had been parked in your way, you would have kept walking and the truck would have just disintegrated. Or tried to have your babies."

For the first time in a dozen years, Léo doubted his grasp of the English language. The disjointed rambling was oddly… endearing, but what, exactly, was Ben saying? He decided to ignore most of it and focus on the goal.

"What does that have to do with my wallet?" he asked, and then winced as Ben sipped from his glass again.

"You didn't have it. The other guy did. Satchel man. He gave it to you, and you put it in your pocket—but then it was in the other pocket! Like magic." His eyes widened, and he leaned forward, almost falling off the stool. "Are you a magician?"

"No," Léo said, catching him and propping him against the bar so he wouldn't slip again. "I think I understand now. Do you see those men?" He turned and gestured across the room to Karim and Malik. Ben squinted in that direction and nodded. "Those are my cousins, Malik and Karim. Karim is visiting from Saudi Arabia. His father—my uncle—has always spoiled him, and he is not very sensible when it comes to money, so my uncle designated his—" Léo hesitated. People often reacted oddly to the word bodyguard. "—his traveling companion as the keeper of funds. That was the man who gave me the wallet. He didn't want to come to the casino, and so Karim's money was entrusted to me for the evening."

"Ohhhhhhh," Ben said, nodding enthusiastically. "That makes so much sense. And it's so much better than if you were a mafioso." He squinted across the room again. "Although it's kind of not fair that you have his money and he's over there without it."

Léo smiled. "I gave the wallet to Malik before I came to introduce myself. He'll make sure Karim doesn't spend too much money."

"Is Malik visiting from Saudi Arabia too?" Ben tipped his head to the side, and his whole body leaned precariously as he continued to watch Léo's cousins.

"No, Malik and I live here, in Monaco."

Ben's big brown eyes blinked. "But you said you were

French." He sounded utterly confused. "Doesn't that mean you live in France?"

Léo chuckled. "Sometimes I do," he admitted. "I was born in France, raised there, and consider myself French. But for most of the year, I live here. I find the weather and lifestyle to my liking."

Ben sighed. "Okay. Is Malik French too? Only his name doesn't sound French like yours."

Léo raised an eyebrow. "You're very curious, aren't you?"

"I like to know things," Ben said, nodding. When his head continued to bob, Léo decided it would be performing a public service to feed the bunny and soak up some of the alcohol in his system.

"Have you dined this evening?" he asked. Ben stopped nodding and moved his head in an odd manner that Léo interpreted as a cross between a shake and a nod.

"I had the best ice cream!" Ben declared. "That's when I saw you—when I was finishing my ice cream. Have you had ice cream at the Café de Paris? You should. It's really amazing." His gaze unfocused as he seemed to remember the ice cream, and Léo's dick hardened at the sight of the dreamy expression, combined with the memory of his bunny's pink tongue licking a spoon.

"I have," he said hoarsely and then cleared his throat. "You had nothing more than ice cream?"

"I had a sandwich this afternoon," he offered helpfully.

"Well,"—Léo stood and gestured for the bartender— "will you do me the honor of your company at dinner? They have a fair restaurant here." He told the bartender to send the remaining champagne to the restaurant—he did not need to specify which one—and helped Ben off the stool.

"Dinner?" Ben asked. He looked at his watch, swaying slightly. "It's kind of late."

"If you say so," Léo murmured. "Supper, then?"

Ben shrugged and smiled widely, and again Léo found himself captivated by his utter openness. "Sure. Let's have supper. I've never had supper before," he confided just a little too loudly as Léo guided him toward the door. The sound of Malik's laughter reached him, and a quick glance proved that his cousin's amusement was indeed at his expense. Karim looked a little startled, and Léo remembered that he hadn't told the boy he was gay. Oh well, Malik could handle it.

Ben chattered without artifice about his ice cream as they made their way through the casino to Le Train Bleu. A young couple, obviously tourists, was just turning away from the entrance as they approached.

"Don't bother unless you have a reservation," the man told them in a broad American accent as they passed.

Ben stumbled to a halt. "Oh, what a shame," he said, sounding genuinely disappointed.

"Why?" Léo asked, taking his hand and tugging him forward. The maître d'hôtel smiled at him.

"Bonsoir, Monsieur Artois," he greeted, then led them to a table. Ben muttered something that Léo didn't bother trying to hear.

Once they were settled and the remainder of their champagne had been delivered and poured, Ben set his menu down and focused on Léo.

"Did you have a reservation?"

Léo picked up his menu. "No."

Bunny frowned, a line appearing between his eyebrows. "So how did we just walk in and get a table?"

He scanned the fish options and decided against them. "I don't need a reservation." As the silence stretched a little too long, he looked up. Ben was staring at him with an expression Léo did not like, a mix of repulsion and shock. "What's wrong? Are you feeling sick?"

"You don't need a reservation?"

Léo frowned in confusion. "No. Are you okay?"

"So you can just walk into any restaurant and demand a table, and you get it? What happens if all the tables are taken? Do they make someone leave halfway through their meal?"

"I have no idea," Léo said, taken aback. He'd never thought about it. When he wanted to eat out, he went to a restaurant and they gave him a table. But Ben was glaring at him now, obviously considering this to be of some importance, and Léo decided to placate him. "Next time I go to a restaurant, I will ensure nobody is discommoded on my behalf."

Ben snickered. "Discommoded." Then he went back to his glare. "Somehow I don't think they'd turn you away." Finally, his gaze dropped to the menu. "Oh good, it's in English. Holy cow, this place ain't cheap. I really don't want to spend this much on supper. I don't even know what supper really is."

Bemused, Léo shook his head. "I issued the invitation, Ben. You are my guest for this meal."

Bunny chewed on his lower lip again, and Léo shifted uncomfortably in his chair. He really wanted to lick that lip.

"I don't know...," Ben murmured, and Léo seized control of the situation.

"I insist. New experiences, remember?"

"Oh yeah." Ben looked back at his menu. "In that case, I should probably choose something really different to eat, right? But I don't want anything like brains or tripe. I tried snails when I was in France, and they weren't bad, mostly just garlicky, but not really something I'd want to eat regularly. But they don't have them here anyway," he said, frowning.

"Would you like me to order for you?" Léo offered. He'd swung between being annoyed, amused, and charmed by Ben so many times that he felt faintly dizzy.

"Please." Ben put down his menu and smiled, and Léo decided "charmed" was going to win.

He ordered for them both and tried not to cringe when Ben reached for his champagne. "Perhaps wait to drink that with the meal," he suggested as tactfully as he could manage. "Unless you'd like wine with your food?"

Ben set the glass down hastily. "Um, no. No wine. This is perfect. Um. Thank you." He flushed again. "Wow, I sound like a moron, don't I? Don't worry, I'm fully aware that this champagne has made me a real dork, and tomorrow I'm going to die of embarrassment. Thank you for being so nice." He paused. "Um… why are you being so nice?"

Léo chuckled. "Maybe I'm a nice person."

Ben nodded hastily. "Sure, sure, nice person. Definitely. I mean, you're being nice to me, so you must be, right? But even nice people don't usually spend a small fortune on strangers who have feet permanently stuck in their mouths."

Léo's gaze dropped to that lower lip, a little puffy from Ben's mistreatment. "I like your mouth." His voice was just a tiny bit deeper than usual. Ben's eyes widened. The moment drew out.

"So. Um. You were going to tell me why Malik doesn't have a French name."

With a chuckle, Léo let him redirect the conversation. "Was I?"

"Yes," Ben said firmly, meeting Léo's gaze but twiddling his thumbs.

"Very well. It's quite simple, really. Malik doesn't have a French name because he's not French."

Ben laughed. "That is simple, and answers my question, but tells me nothing."

"Malik's mother and mine are sisters—twins, actually. My aunt married a local man in Saudi Arabia, but my mother met my father, who is a Frenchman, when she was shopping in Paris, and after many family histrionics on both sides, married him. Hence Malik being Malik, and me being Léo."

"That's so cool, your parents falling in love like that and overcoming parental disapproval," Ben enthused.

Léo huffed. "Love? Hardly. They are fond of each other, but their decision to marry was based more on the ability to meet mutual wants than anything else."

Ben's mouth turned down. "You just see it that way because they're your parents. Most kids don't see their parents as romantic."

"No. I see it that way because that's how they explained it to me when I was twenty-one and refusing to fall in with their plans for me."

"Oh." Ben fiddled with his cutlery, and Léo decided a change of subject was in order. He disliked talking about his family situation at the best of times, and while his goal here was not to make Ben his confidant, he also didn't want him feeling uncomfortable.

No, he wanted him nice and relaxed.

"Where are you from, Ben?"

Bunny looked up with a smile. "Australia. Melbourne, actually."

"A very nice city," Léo offered. "I was there for the

Grand Prix three or four years ago. What brings you to Europe? Just a holiday?"

"Sort of. I'm visiting all the places Mrs. K. loved."

The waiter served their food then, and Léo waited for him to leave before asking, "Mrs. K.?"

"Oh, she was my last client. I'm a nurse, see. Mrs. K.'s family hired me to look after her after her stroke. She was really great, and we had a few years together. I really miss her. When she was younger, she loved to travel, and she told me all about the places she'd been and things she'd done—and she'd done a lot. She'd tell me to take advantage of my youth and do everything I wanted to do while I still could. And then she died and left me some money, so I decided to go on a trip in tribute to her." Ben blinked fiercely. "She really loved Monaco, so even though it's not somewhere I'd ever planned to come, I had to add it to my list."

Léo lifted his glass. It seemed Bunny had hidden depths —not everyone was willing to leave money to an employee, and not all employees would use that money in tribute. Léo felt oddly warm at the thought.

"To your Mrs. K., then. May her adventures continue."

Chapter Three

He was going to kill his phone.

The shrill sound—*who picked that stupid ringtone anyway?*—would not stop. Or rather, it had stopped twice, and then started again immediately. He knew only one person who was stubborn and annoying enough to ring three times in a row without leaving a message, interrupting the most delicious dream about a handsome, wealthy Frenchman who flirted with him.

Ben emerged from his cocoon of pillows—bless the Fairmont and their generous pillow allotment—and snatched the phone from the bedside table, swiping at the screen.

"What?" he snarled.

"Rise and shine! Why are you wasting the morning? The internet says you have a beautiful day there, and you should be making the most of it—or at least soaking up the sunshine by the gorgeous rooftop pool the hotel website boasts about. Isn't there a DJ up there?"

Ben shoved the pillows behind him and leaned back, sliding down in the bed a bit. "How do you know I'm not already by the pool or sightseeing, only to be interrupted by your inability to leave a damn message?"

His best friend, Danika, laughed. "I just know, Benji. Now tell me all about your first day in Monaco."

"I wish you'd stop calling me that. My name's not even Benjamin," Ben grumbled, and squinted at the other side of the bed in the low light. Was that a piece of paper?

"Sorry, Ben-e-dict. Seriously, what was your mother thinking? Benedict. Nobody in Australia is called Benedict." Ben was only half listening as he wiggled in his nest of pillows, trying to reach the paper without having to move too much.

"Aha!" He snatched it up triumphantly.

"What? Ben, are you even listening to me?"

"Not really," he said, scowling. It was too dim in the room with the drapes closed to read the paper. Damn upmarket hotels with their fancy blackout curtains. He shuffled back toward the bedside table and flipped on the lamp.

Then froze.

"Oh my fuck."

Memory flooded in.

A handsome, wealthy Frenchman.

Flirting.

With him.

Plying him with astronomically expensive champagne.

Buying him dinner.

Sipping a digestif with him on a moonlit terrace over-looking the ocean.

Walking him back to his hotel.

Kissing him....

What the fuck did I do?

"Ben! *Benedict!* Answer me right now, or I'll call hotel reception and have them check on you!"

"I'm here," he said numbly.

Dani sighed heavily. "Thank God! You can't just swear and then go silent like that when you're on the other side of the world."

"Sorry."

Silence. Ben stared at the note in his hand, at the perfect penmanship so unlike his own scrawl. The neatly spaced words.

"Ben?" Dani's voice was quiet. "What's wrong?"

Ben swallowed. "I don't know."

"Oh-kay. Are you hurt?"

Ben assessed. Aside from being thirsty, he felt pretty good. No hangover, probably thanks to Léo feeding him. "No. Not hurt."

"Sick, then?" Dani was starting to sound impatient, now that he'd told her he was okay.

"I'm not sick. Sorry, Dani. I think I might have done something stupid, but I'm not sure."

Pause.

"Not sure if you did it, or not sure if it was stupid?"

Ben blinked. "Both, actually."

"Well… stupid things on holidays usually involve alcohol, drugs, or sex. I know you don't do drugs, ever, so that's out."

Ben sighed. "I met this guy." The silence drew out, and he frowned. "Dani?"

"I'm here. Wow. I thought it would be alcohol."

He chuckled. "It was."

Dani gasped. "Did someone get you drunk and take advantage of you? Do you need a doctor? Are you somewhere safe?"

His heart warmed. If he said the word, Dani would leap on a plane and come to his rescue, he just knew it. "I'm fine, Dani. I'm in my hotel room, alone, and…." He shifted experimentally in the bed, just to make sure. He remembered Léo kissing him good night and leaving, but it didn't hurt to be certain. "Nobody took advantage of me."

"Then you better start talking, Benji, because I've got a whole lot of questions and no information."

Ben sighed again. "Okay, but let me tell it all before you start giving opinions."

"Fine."

"I was having ice cream at the Café de Paris—"

"The place Mrs. K. told you to go?"

"Yes. Amazing, by the way. The ice cream was incredible. Anyway, I'd just finished, and these guys walked across the square to the casino."

"Hot guys, obviously. OMG, were you in an orgy?" Dani squealed.

"No orgy. And never say OMG again. And is this letting me tell it?"

"Sorry." She didn't sound at all apologetic, so Ben let his silence linger for a long moment. "I swear, I'm sorry! I won't interrupt."

"Okay." Ben took his time describing the sensations of utter lust and insatiable curiosity he'd felt, knowing Dani wouldn't understand if he just said he'd followed the men (*and* gone back to the hotel to change clothes) for the hell of it. She knew him too well. She was mostly silent, only chuckling a little as he related what an utter moron he'd been when Léo had introduced himself in the Salle Blanche. Ben would have chuckled himself, but he was too busy cringing over his shocked reaction to having the man he'd been searching for approach *him*.

She outright laughed when she heard that Ben had called Léo both a con man and a member of the Albanian mafia—oh, and a magician. He sidetracked slightly to wax lyrical over the champagne, taking a moment to remember the taste of it on his tongue, nothing like the champagne he was used to avoiding.

She made intrigued noises when he told her about Malik and Karim, and a mixture of impressed and derisive ones over the whole "I don't need a reservation" scenario.

"We sat and talked over supper for two hours, Dani. I can't remember the last time I talked to a stranger for more than two minutes. Or anyone other than you."

"What is supper, anyway?" Dani asked. "Is it dinner? Or is it like a postdinner thing?"

Ben laughed. "I looked it up. In this context, it's a light meal late in the evening."

"Oh. But do you have dinner as well? Or is it like a late dinner?" Dani's tone had that edge of curiosity that meant she'd fixate on this until she had an answer.

"I honestly don't know," he told her. "I just popped my supper cherry last night, remember?" He paused. "Please forget I said that."

"It was kind of yuck," she agreed. "Okay, so this incredibly hot man with oodles of sex appeal has bought you champagne that you never even dreamed about, whisked you off for *supper* in a fully booked restaurant, and connected with you well enough that you were able to talk for hours. This sounds kinda like a movie."

"There's more," Ben said gloomily, depressed at the thought that his life could be a rom com. Knowing his luck, there would be a nasty twist and it would turn out it was all for a bet, or that he'd inadvertently seen something top secret and Léo was an assassin sent to silence him. "I don't want to die before I see Italy."

To her credit, Dani only hesitated for a second before their brains synced and she got it. "You'd know if you'd seen something worth being killed for," she pointed out.

"Or Léo would have killed you already. Let's face it, you wouldn't exactly be hard to murder."

"Hey, I work out!" he said indignantly. "I'm strong. Nurses have to lift things all the time. I have *lean muscle.*"

"I know, I just meant— Wait. Let's talk about that later. Tell me about the 'more' you mentioned."

"What more?" Ben was still morosely contemplating the possibility that Léo had slipped some kind of slow-acting poison into the champagne, and that the best drink of his life was actually going to kill him. *I don't even regret it.*

"I summarized your amazing evening, and you said 'there's more.' Tell me about the more," Dani insisted, dragging him out of his fond reminiscence of the champagne that cost more than his first car.

"Oh. Well, we were still in the restaurant, and the waiter came and asked if we wanted a digestif."

"What's a digestif? And if you tell me you didn't have to look it up, I won't believe you."

"I didn't, but only because I asked Léo. It's an after-dinner alcoholic drink. It's supposed to help you digest. Get it? Digestif."

"Why can't they just call it an after-dinner drink?"

Ben let his head fall back against the pillows. "How the fuck do I know? I only learned about it last night, and I'd already drunk two-thirds of a bottle of champagne by then."

"Fine. Continue."

Ben pulled the phone away from his ear and glared at it, then reluctantly put it back.

"Did you just make a face at the phone?" Dani asked.

"Yes. Anyway, I said I'd never had a digestif before, like the completely unsophisticated dolt I am, and Léo said in that case, we should go back to the Salle Blanche and have our digestif on the terrace. So we did. On a moonlit terrace overlooking the ocean."

"Whoa! Léo has some smooth moves."

"Right? So I'm full of great food and alcohol—I don't even want to look up how much the digestif cost, because it was some kind of fortified wine, but no wine I ever drank tasted that good—and I'm sitting on a terrace with the sound of the ocean not far off, with this guy who breaks the hotness meter, and I'm thinking the night can't get better."

"And…?"

"And I didn't want to chance everything going downhill, so I said I wanted to go back to my hotel."

"Ben!"

"Not like that," he assured her hastily. "I didn't say it like that, and he didn't take it like that."

"Humph." Dani wasn't usually a prude—she had more one-nighters under her belt than he did—but she'd made him promise before he'd left that he wouldn't do anything risky when she was too far away to come to his rescue. Just in case. "So then what?"

"He walked me back to the hotel. We went the long way around, and… it's hard to describe. From the square where the casino is, the Fairmont is down a really steep hill. So the best way to access the hotel is from the rooftop pool area. And he stops me beside the pool, which is softly lit and quiet, and he put his hand on my face…." Ben drifted into a daydream. Léo's kiss had been both fiercely hot and lazily sexy. His hands had been firm on Ben's body, wandering up and down his back, brushing over his arse… and he was a hell of a kisser. Just enough tongue, not sloppy or too dry. It was the kind of kiss Ben could get lost in, his awareness of details blurring until everything was heat and mouth and hard body against his, silky-soft hair under his hands, floating away on lust.... He'd come out of it unsure how much time had passed and which way was up.

Dani cleared her throat, dragging Ben back to the present, his face hot and his dick half-hard. "Right, so he kissed you in a romantic setting... and by the sounds of it, knocked your socks off. Then...?"

Ben coughed lightly, suddenly embarrassed. "Well, then the alcohol must have hit me, because I was kind of unsteady. Maybe I took a step back, and he had to grab me before I fell in the pool." Dani's laughter was totally expected, but Ben almost didn't care, because Léo's arms had been as strong as steel and yet so gentle as he snatched Ben back from the edge of the pool. *Am I gushing like a Disney princess? I am. Crap.*

"Sure," she said between chuckles. "It was the alcohol."

"Anyway," Ben soldiered on, "he walked me up to my room. And it really was the alcohol, because I made a complete arse of myself." He glared at the note still in his hand.

"What do you mean? What did you do? Trip over your own feet?"

"How many times do I have to tell you, the carpet was lumpy! Anyway," he drew the word out, "I didn't trip over anything. He walked me up to my room, waited until I opened the door. I asked him in... to translate something in the hotel directory."

"I thought everyone spoke English in Monaco? Well, apart from the doormen at the casino, obviously. But the Fairmont is a big hotel. Didn't they have an English trans — Ohhhhhh. Right. To translate."

Ben's cheeks burned, even though Dani was half a

world away and would probably have encouraged the action had she known about it beforehand.

"So he came in, and he had this little smile, and I knew he knew I didn't need anything translated, but I was feeling kinda loose and I didn't care." He winced a little at the memory. In retrospect, Léo's attitude had been rather indulgent at that point, not that of a man who was panting with lust for him.

"Because of the alcohol, and the fact that he was majorly hot and the whole night was like a fairy tale."

"Right. But then I throw myself at him—maybe kind of literally—and he kisses me, and it got really hot. Like, *really* hot." He paused. Even as a nurse, he hadn't known body temperature could go up that quickly purely because of a kiss and some groping. Léo hadn't been just indulging him *then*. There had been some actual panting, and not all from Ben. "And then he tells me to get into the bed, and I'm all hell yeah, so I strip and get under the covers."

"This isn't going to be a tell-all, is it?" Dani interrupted. "Because I thought we stopped doing that years ago."

"There's nothing to tell," Ben said glumly. "I'd pretty much just gotten settled in the bed, and he walks over, kisses me on the forehead, and tells me he'll see me for lunch. Then he left."

"He *left*?" Her incredulity was a balm to his ego. "He left guaranteed sex with a drunk tourist?"

"Hey!"

"Ben, what part of my sentence was untrue?"

Ben ran it back through his mind and sighed because it was all true. "Fine. Yes, he left guaranteed sex with a drunk tourist."

"That's really kind of sweet," Dani tried to console

him. "He knew you'd had too much to drink, and he didn't take advantage of that. And wait, did you say lunch?"

"Yep," Ben told her, slightly cheered by her perspective. It *was* sweet, damn it. Léo had to kind of like and respect him, or he wouldn't have bothered, right? "He actually meant it too. I found a note on my bed. That's why I swore before, by the way."

"He left you a note? Oh man, has this guy got the moves. What does it say?"

Ben lifted the paper again. He'd read it about a dozen times already, but still the sight of Léo's handwriting made his stomach flip.

"It says he's not sure if I'll remember about lunch, and so he's leaving the note to remind me. One o'clock in the hotel foyer."

"I can't believe he wants to see you again."

"Danika!"

"Well, come on. You were a complete dork. And I mean, if he's as good-looking as you say, and obviously wealthy— Hey, you're in Europe."

Ben blinked. "Yeah. And have been for a while. You know this, you helped me plan the trip, remember?"

"No, I just mean, they have a lot of paparazzi in Europe, right? Who like to take pictures of wealthy people? Especially the good-looking ones. I wanna see if I can find his picture. What's his name again?"

"Dani—"

"C'mon, I've got Google open. Don't pretend you think this is creepy when you once hid in actual bushes to get a look at one of my dates."

Ben sighed. He had done that. "Léonard Artois."

"How do you spell that?"

"What makes you think I know?"

"Never mind, I've— Holy fuck!"

He smiled smugly. "Told you."

"Crap, Benji, you know I love you more than life, but this guy is… holy fuck."

"I know. Don't call me Benji." He contemplated the note. Superhot, sweet, rich… could a guy like that be real? "Maybe I shouldn't go to lunch."

"Holy fuck!"

He frowned. "You've already said that."

"No, I'm reading his Wikipedia page."

Ben dropped the note and sat bolt upright. "He has a *Wikipedia page*? What for?"

"For being hideously gorgeous and wealthy and a playboy loved by the paparazzi."

"I'll call you back, I need—"

"No fucking way. I'll tell you the good bits. Right. Léonard Khalid Artois. Twenty-nine years old."

"I thought he was older," Ben murmured.

"He doesn't look older," Dani said, obviously leering at photos of Léo.

"No, but he seems… I don't know. Mature. Sophisticated."

"Did you know his mother is a princess?"

"*What?*"

"Well, the daughter of a Saudi prince. That makes her a princess, right? But his grandfather's not in line for a throne or anything, unless about nine thousand people die in a really short space of time."

"Are you fucking kidding me right now?" Ben slumped back on the pillows and stared at the ceiling. Léo's mother was a princess.

"Not kidding. I'll swear on anything you want."

"Fuck me."

"No, honey, you don't like girls, remember?" Dani's smirk was evident in her voice, and if she'd been there, Ben would have thrown a pillow at her.

"What else?" he asked grimly.

"Well, the French side of the family is pretty much as exalted as the Saudi side. Like, they can trace their ancestors back for lots of hundreds of years. He's got an older brother who works with their father doing... wow, that's a lot of businesses and industries. Basically, they've got lots of fingers in lots of pies. Property all over Europe, especially in France, and quite a few of them belong just to your honey, not the family."

"Great," Ben muttered. He'd known Léo had money, but... crap. No wonder he could buy higher-than-top-shelf champagne for dorky tourists and get a table at any restaurant he wanted.

"Léo's always been kind of a wild child, though. He and his cousin Malik—ooh, there's a link to a page for him too, we'll go back to that later—anyway, they were both kicked out of the best schools in France. That's schools, plural. Then they went to England for uni—Oxford, no less."

"He told me he and Malik studied in England." Ben sighed. For all that Léo had said a lot, it seemed more had been left out.

"He and Malik seem kinda attached at the hip, to be honest. Since they graduated—both near the top of the class, so they either got smarts, or they used some of their cash to buy their way through school... what was I saying?"

"Since they graduated," Ben prompted, wondering if it was too early to hit the minibar. It was five o'clock somewhere, right?

"Oh yeah. They spent a few years on the move, basically going from party to party, before they settled in Monaco about five years ago. They still hit the social scene pretty hard, but not so much the crazy parties anymore."

Well, that's… whatever. "What does he do?" Ben asked.

"What do you mean? I just told you, he lives the high life all over Europe."

"No, for a job. Like, what does he do every day? Does he work with his dad and brother?"

Dani paused. "Honey, Léo's a wealthy European play-boy. He has more money than you or I can even believe exists. He doesn't work. He just… bums around."

"He bums around." Ben hadn't thought he could get more depressed, but as someone with a strong work ethic who'd started working part-time at fifteen and had had a job since, the idea of "bumming around" *all the time* was anathema to him.

"Don't be judgmental, Benji. If he worked, he could be taking a job from someone who actually needed it to feed their family."

"So he does volunteer stuff or something?" Ben asked hopefully.

Dani's silence was deafening.

"Right." He sighed. "Well, it's not like I ever thought he was my Prince Charming, right? And he gave me a great night. An experience. A story to tell."

"Whoa, mate. You're talking like you're not going to see him again. Lunch, remember?"

Ben grimaced. "Yeah, I don't think I'll do that, Dani. What's the point? It's not like it can ever lead anywhere. I leave in four days."

"Exactly! Ben, this is your chance to have a fling with a wealthy European playboy! It'll be an adventure to tell people about when you get old, about the time in Monaco you were picked up by the half-French son of a Saudi princess and romanced by moonlight, wooed with champagne, and then had intense, crazy sex with for just a few days before you waved goodbye and swanned off to Italy for your next adventure. How many people can say they did that?"

Ben wavered. She had a point. It would make for a fabulous story. Mrs. K. would have loved it. Plus, it would mean he could see Léo again. *Have sex* with Léo. Gorgeous, sexy Léo, who made him feel interesting and desirable and not dorky even when he was. He could be saying the dumbest thing and know that he'd feel like an idiot later, but the look in Léo's dark-as-sin eyes just made him feel sexy and adorable.

"Dani?" he said as he kicked back the covers and climbed out of bed.

"Yeah?" She sounded wary.

"What the hell am I going to wear?"

Chapter Four

On Dani's orders, Ben had a light snack at eleven, even though he hadn't eaten breakfast until after nine. "What if he orders wine with lunch?" she'd asked practically. "You don't want to drink on an empty stomach again. He probably already thinks you're a lightweight."

After that heartwarming assessment, he'd been forced to go through the contents of his suitcase in detail. It had been a depressing experience. Ben liked being casual, and the only clothes he'd brought along that weren't "too shabby" were the trousers and shirt he'd worn the night before—which Dani deemed unacceptable, as Léo had seen them. Ben's horrified exclamation that he was *not* buying new clothes had been brushed aside, and after a quick shower and a more leisurely breakfast—leisurely just to spite Dani, who was waiting in Australia for him to finish—he found himself taking his phone (and thus Dani) shopping.

His BFF believed, as he did, that a belt should not cost as much as rent, and so had spent her wait time frantically searching the internet for a reasonably priced clothing store near him. She'd had no luck, so Ben, phone plastered to his ear, took himself off to ask the concierge for help. At first he'd worried that a language barrier was causing the man to look at him so oddly, but it turned out just to be general disbelief that a guest of the Fairmont was asking for a discount shopping outlet. Once he came to terms with it, he was as helpful as possible, mentioning a market in a small town on the Italian border, only twenty or so minutes away by train. Dani nixed that idea, claiming he didn't have time to get there, shop, and get back with still enough time to make himself presentable, especially as there was no guarantee he'd find something suitable. Ben was vaguely insulted by the insinuation that he needed a lot of time to look presentable, but let that go in favor of arguing about her latest edict that he had to suck it up and buy designer.

The concierge interjected at that point, advising that he was likely to find some "not too expensive" designer stores at Le Metropole Shopping Center. Ben took his advice, waved off the ridiculous offer of a taxi in favor of walking the very short distance, and then nearly suffered a heart attack upon arrival at Le Metropole when he saw exactly what the concierge considered not too expensive. A whispered argument with Dani and a promise that he'd never again need to buy her a Christmas present resulted in him marching stiff-backed into the nearest store that sold men's clothing and spending the next twenty minutes hunting through the displays while he muttered into his phone and two wary salespeople watched him. Finally, he gave up searching for a bargain and, with Dani yammering in his ear, requested assistance.

"Oui, monsieur," the young man, whose name tag said Michel, agreed—albeit cautiously. Apparently they didn't often get people in old shorts with their toe poking out of their shoe in that store. Or maybe it was the fact that Dani could actually be heard through the phone, her voice tinny and yet still shrill as she told Ben exactly what he needed. The other salesperson, a young woman, disappeared into the back of the store.

"I have a lunch date and I need something to wear," Ben said. "The voice you hear is my friend in Australia, who doesn't think I'm capable of shopping on my own."

Michel's gaze swept over Ben from head to toe (literally), and from his expression, Ben guessed he agreed with Dani.

"We can help," Michel assured. "This lunch, is it casual? Or something more chic?"

"I have no idea," Ben told him. "Here"—he fished the note from Léo out of his pocket and handed it over—"this is everything I know."

The salesman frowned at the piece of paper before handing it back. In Ben's ear, Dani demanded to speak with him. Ben sighed.

"Brace yourself," he warned, and then handed over the phone. Michel took it warily, but within moments was smiling and nodding, making sweeping gestures as he spoke, as though Dani could see him.

Ben wished them both to perdition.

"Alors," Michel said finally, handing Ben back his phone. "I know just what you need." He immediately began bustling around the store, pausing only briefly to scan Ben again before he started piling clothes on the counter. Ben eyed the growing stack dubiously.

"Dani," he interrupted whatever she was babbling about. "Why is this man choosing me an entire new wardrobe?"

Michel called out, and the saleswoman emerged from

the back of the store and began carrying the pile of clothes to a change room.

"Benji, let's face it, you don't have the wardrobe for Monaco, and you definitely don't have the wardrobe to date a sophisticated, hot billionaire. So you're just going to have to buy one."

"Are you *insane*?" Ben hissed. "Do you know how much these clothes cost?" He snagged a shirt from the display nearest to him and looked at the discreet tag. "Holy fu—"

"Don't you dare swear in that shop!" Dani demanded.

"Why not? Rich people swear, you know." Sometimes she said the dumbest things. "Dani, I'm holding a cotton T-shirt that costs nearly two hundred and fifty Australian dollars. For a T-shirt! I can't afford a new wardrobe from this place."

"Well, technically, you can."

Ben returned the shirt to the display. She was right, damn her. "Let me put it this way, then—I don't want to pay that much money for clothes."

"Please, Ben? You can't go to lunch, or to anything else Léo might plan, wearing Target-brand T-shirts you found secondhand at the Salvos store. And you told me that your runners were on the verge of falling apart." Ben glared down at his big toe where it so cheekily peeked out of his shoe. "Buy a couple of outfits. Enough to get through the next few days. When you get to Italy, pack them up and put them at the bottom of your suitcase. We'll sell them on eBay or Gumtree when you get home. Hardly worn designer stuff holds its value."

Across the store, Michel beckoned eagerly. Ben tried really hard not to glare at him.

"Are you sure?" he asked.

"Cross my heart. You'll get a lot of the money back."

Ben sighed. He was pretty sure she wasn't telling him

the truth. But he could technically afford it, thanks to Mrs. K., and it had been a really long time since he'd bought new clothes that were actually new. Why not splurge?

Which was how he came to be sitting in the foyer at the Fairmont, dressed in formfitting caramel-colored trousers and a pale blue polo shirt, with what he was pretty sure were blue boat shoes on his feet. Boat. Shoes. What the hell had happened to him? The entire outfit, including brown leather belt, had cost about as much as the bottle of champagne Léo had bought the night before.

Léo. It was kind of sappy, and he'd never say it out loud to anyone, not even Dani—especially not Dani—but trying to appeal to Léo was kind of worth the money and hassle.

Crap, he was *such* a dork.

And on the topic of his dorkiness, was it really sad and lame that he was sitting here waiting right by the door? Should he go back up to his room and come down a few minutes after one?

Ben leaped to his feet, nearly slamming into a passing hotel guest, and after profuse apologies hurried toward the lifts. Halfway there, he decided pretending to be late was just as lame as being eagerly early, so he changed direction abruptly and went over to one of the shops in the foyer, peering in the window and pretending to be fascinated by the display while he actually watched the reflection in the glass of the doors behind him. It took him a few minutes— and the glare of the saleswoman in the store—to realize he was "staring" at a women's swimwear display. His face went hot and he took two quick steps back—

And collided with a warm body. A hard body. One that smelled so good.

Of course Léo would be witness to yet another embarrassing moment.

Ben slowly turned around and smiled weakly. "Hey."

Léo's amused smile melted his insides. Without the concern about his identity or the buffer of alcohol, lust hit hard and sharply. Today, the demigod was wearing an outfit similar to his own, only his shirt was red, a color that did amazing things for Léo's dark skin and eyes. Ben's cock jerked in his too-tight trousers, trying to sit up and beg.

"Good afternoon," Léo said, and Christ, how had Ben not noticed how amazing his voice was? It was like coconut rough, if coconut rough were a voice, or voices could be chocolate. It vibrated through every cell in Ben's body, the warm, deep timbre stroking over—

"Ben?" From the questioning tone, it wasn't the first time Léo had said his name. Ben hadn't thought it was possible for his cheeks to get hotter, but it seemed he was wrong.

"Er, sorry. Um. Distracted. Remembering… stuff. That I need to do. But not right now!" he rushed to assure Léo. "Now I'm all yours. For lunch. I mean, to have lunch with." He fell silent, wishing fervently that he had a time machine and could redo the last ten minutes. Sitting by the door eagerly was suddenly a much more sensible option.

"I'm glad you are all mine for lunch," Léo murmured, with a hot look that couldn't be misunderstood. Ben was sure his heart actually *stopped beating*.

"Ungh…."

"What would you like for lunch?" Léo asked. "Have you eaten here at the hotel yet? The main restaurant is only open for dinner, but the restaurant upstairs is decent. Or we could go to the club."

"The club?" Ben asked blankly. Like a nightclub? That served lunch?

"The yacht club," Léo told him. "They have a nice bistro there for casual meals."

Ben's eyes went wide. He'd never been to a yacht club —didn't even know anyone who had a yacht, although maybe now he did—but his image of one was based on many movies, and he was sure it wasn't a place he'd fit well. The "casual" hotel restaurant, on the other hand, he'd walked past several times, and it looked quite comfortable, even if he hadn't wanted to spend that much on meals while he was here.

"Let's eat here," he said quickly. "I haven't tried the restaurant yet, but I saw the menu and it looks good."

Léo smiled in a way that made Ben's stomach feel funny, and in short order they were at the mostly open-air restaurant on the roof level, greeted effusively by a man who seated them at what Ben was sure was the best table in the place, shaded yet with an uninterrupted view of the Mediterranean.

If he hadn't been so stupidly nervous, Ben would have soaked it up.

The maître d'hôtel left them, replaced by an eager waiter who asked what they wanted to drink. Léo shot Ben a wicked glance, his lips curving, and Ben's face went hot.

"Sparkling water," Léo told the waiter. "Then perhaps wine later." The man left, and Ben smiled gratefully at Léo.

"Thank you," he said. "And thank you for being so good about last night. I know I made a bit of a fool of myself."

"Not at all," Léo said gallantly. "You were charming."

Ben laughed outright. "I wouldn't have called it that, but hey, your description sounds better than mine. Anyway, I drank too much of that incredible champagne, and you were really nice. So thanks."

Léo's expression was warm and approving. "I'm glad you enjoyed the champagne, and it was my pleasure to spend the evening with you. We would not be here now otherwise."

Ben's face went hot again, and he buried it in his menu. He felt awkward, even more than usual, and desperately wanted the loosening effects of alcohol. Maybe he should have ordered a drink, after all, but he didn't want Léo to think he was a lush.

Come on, Ben. You don't need alcohol to talk to the billionaire playboy son of a princess.

Fuck. He needed to come up with a safe topic of conversation, something that would allow him to be intelligent and witty—or at least not a total loser—and woo Léo into his bed.

The waiter came back with their water, and hovered, ready to take their order. Léo ordered his meal decisively and then cast an inquisitive glance at Ben, who wished he had the nerve to ask Léo to order for him like he had the night before. Instead, he randomly picked a pasta dish, and felt first relief, then shame at his relief, when Léo ordered a bottle of wine to have with lunch. *I'll only have one glass*, he promised himself. One glass with a meal wouldn't affect him, but he could convince his brain that it had and hopefully relax enough to hold up his end of a rational conversation.

The waiter left, and silence stretched between them. Each second lasted an eternity, going on and on and—

"Oxford!" Ben blurted, then mentally kicked himself.

Léo blinked. "Oxford?"

"You went there," Ben continued, wondering when he'd lost the ability to construct a sentence. He took a deep breath and made himself smile. "I visited when I was in England, and I thought it was amazing." There, that was pretty good. "What was it like to study there?" He sat back, proud of himself. He'd started a conversation.

"I enjoyed it," Léo said, "although how much of that was due to the locale and how much was due to the pubs is up for debate."

Ben laughed, fondly remembering his own uni days and frequent piss-ups at the local pub. He was about to make a comment to that effect when Léo spoke again.

"How did you know I studied at Oxford?" he asked, a gleam in his dark eyes that told Ben he knew exactly how and found it amusing to tease him.

"Er…." *Oh, fuck. This is all Dani's fault.* "You told me last night, remember?"

Léo leaned back in his seat, a small smile twitching his lips. "Did I? I thought I'd only said I studied in England, when you asked me why my English was so good."

"No, no, you said you studied at…." Ben gave up. He'd never been much of a liar, and right now his face was so hot that he knew he must be lobster red. He grimaced. "Okay, so maybe I was talking to Dani—my best friend, Danika. Did I mention her?" Léo nodded slightly. "So I was talking to Dani this morning when I saw your note, and I told her about you, and maybe she was curious and googled you and then made me listen while she read your Wikipedia page." He snatched up the glass of sparkling water in front of him and took a gulp, instantly regretting it when the bubbles burned the back of his throat. Eyes watering, he blinked furiously and then gave up and swiped at his eyes. By the time he was finally able to focus again, he felt real tears prickling. Why did he have to be such a dork?

Unable to look up, he kept his gaze on the table. "I'm sorry," he said softly. "We shouldn't have invaded your privacy." He swallowed hard. "If you want to leave, that's fine. I'll sort things out with the waiter."

There was a long moment of silence, and then a big

hand on his face, lifting it so he had no choice but to look at Léo.

"No one is leaving," Léo said, his usually arrogant expression soft. His black eyes met Ben's. "I don't think you can call it an invasion of my privacy if you read it on Wikipedia. It's not as if your Dani was hiding in the bushes outside my window."

Ben's face flamed *again* as he remembered that one time he'd actually hidden in the bushes to scope out the guy Dani had been dating. Léo arched an eyebrow.

"Is there something you haven't told me?" he asked.

After sputtering for a moment, Ben gave up and laughed helplessly. "This may change your mind about me," he warned, and then launched into the story. Léo listened with clear incredulity at first, before amusement took over.

The waiter arrived with their food and wine, and Ben tried not to be obvious about the fact that he snatched up his wineglass as soon as the waiter filled it. He took a sip, thinking that would probably be sufficient to fool his brain into relaxing, but the rich red wine tasted so good that he went back for another mouthful before reluctantly putting the glass down. It was just as well he wasn't planning to settle into this lifestyle. He'd become a drunk very quickly.

"Tell me," Léo asked when the waiter had left, "why didn't Dani come on this trip with you?"

Ben tipped his head as he forked up pasta, which was thankfully good and not made with anything he hated. "We talked about it," he admitted. "I wanted her to, but she didn't feel she could take that much time away from her job and her family. Her grandmother is unwell, and she and her sister and brother take it in turns to help out."

"Ah. But you speak frequently?"

Ben nodded. "Sure. Text, chat, FaceTime, regular

phone calls… I talk to her in some way or another every day, just like at home. This morning she even came shopping with me." He stopped, aghast. No fucking way was he telling Léo about the impromptu shopping trip to Le Metropole to buy clothes to impress him. "I needed shoes," he tacked on hastily.

Léo grinned. "And you can't buy shoes without Dani's help?"

"Not according to her," Ben said, then grimaced. "Truthfully, she's not entirely wrong. Shopping is not my strong point."

An arrogant shrug was Léo's response. "Shopping is like anything else. The trouble is that people try to do things they have no skill at. Not everyone would attempt to service their own car, because they lack the skill set. Instead, they hire a professional. The same applies to shopping."

Ben wondered if he was hearing right. "Are you saying we should hire people to shop for us?"

Another shrug. "Why not?"

"So," Ben said slowly, "do you hire people to shop for you?" He picked up his glass and took a small sip. He kept getting these reminders that Léo was a billionaire. And not the kind who liked to wear worn-out clothes and pretend to be ordinary. Léo was a high-society billionaire, the kind that appeared in tabloid magazines.

"When I need something, I call my assistant and he arranges it," Léo said coolly. Ben perked up. An assistant meant a job of some kind, right?

"Your assistant?" he asked. "What does he do? I mean," he hurried on as Léo smirked, "I know he assists you, but with what?" He cringed. "Um…." He looked longingly at his wineglass, but resisted to urge to grab it and gulp.

"Never mind," Léo told him. "I know what you're trying to say. Didn't Wikipedia tell you that?" he teased, and Ben shoved another forkful of pasta into his mouth so he wouldn't have to answer. The knowing expression on Léo's face told him he wasn't fooling anyone.

"When I graduated university, my father transferred a number of business interests and investments into my name, in addition to some I inherited from my grandfather. Jean—my assistant—helps me manage those and also coordinates my travel itineraries and oversees maintenance at my homes. Plus anything else I need. He's also my... I suppose 'agent' is the best word, in Paris."

Homes, Ben thought. Dani had told him that Léo owned properties all over Europe, but for some reason Ben hadn't equated that with homes. He'd vaguely pictured rectangles and cards, as in Monopoly, just words on paper, rather than actual land and houses that needed maintenance and... stuff. Like furniture. They were probably big houses too.

Once again, he wondered what the hell he was doing, lusting after a billionaire.

Grow up, Ben, he told himself. He wasn't planning a lifetime commitment to Léo, something that would require him to come to terms with massive wealth and multiple homes throughout Europe. All he wanted was a few days of company with an interesting, off-the-charts-hot man, and hopefully some incredible sex that would ruin him for all men thereafter. He could then spend the rest of his life fondly remembering his fairy-tale fling.

"Maybe I should get an assistant," he mused, then chuckled. "Probably first I'd need something for them to assist me with." He leaned forward conspiratorially. "Are you ever tempted to send—Jean, was it?" Léo nodded, brows drawn together in curiosity. "Have you ever been tempted to send Jean out to do something completely ridiculous?"

"Such as?" Léo asked, frowning slightly.

"If you have to ask, you haven't," Ben decided. He probably would. He'd think of something utterly stupid and unnecessary, like finding six leaves of identical size but different shape, and just once, he'd ask his assistant to do it. Because he could.

That was why he should never have an assistant.

"Should I be concerned about your silence?" Léo asked, and Ben shook himself out of his daydream about being able to demand someone peel him a grape and actually have them obey. Not that he even wanted his grapes peeled—who peeled grapes?—but the idea was cool.

"Sorry, just…. Yeah. So. You live in Monaco, right?" Léo nodded. "Why? I mean, why not Paris or wherever?"

Léo laid down his knife and fork and took a sip from his glass. "Not many people have asked me that," he said thoughtfully. "My father demands it in a way that requires no response, but most others just assume I am here for lack of motivation to be elsewhere—like Paris."

Ben winced. "Uh, I didn't mean it like that," he rushed out, but Léo waved a hand.

"I know. And in all honesty, that is part of the answer. I'm very fond of Paris, but if I were there, my father would be constantly making demands of me, in the hope that if he kept asking, eventually I would give in and join him and Gabriel—my brother, did Wikipedia mention him?" Ben nodded, although he hadn't known his name. "Yes, well, Gabriel is the epitome of the ideal son, but my father would much prefer to have both his sons in his empire. I cannot stand the idea, so I avoid Paris, except for a few quick visits."

"Your family lives in Paris?" Ben ventured.

Léo shook his head. "Not officially, although my parents and my brother have homes there and spend a great deal of time in them."

"So you live here partly to avoid being sucked into the family business," Ben said, carefully not saying, "so you don't have to work." "What's the other part? And why specifically here? Why not elsewhere in France, or London, or… anywhere else?"

The waiter came to clear their plates, and Léo leaned back in his seat, his thoughtful gaze on Ben.

"I like Monaco," he said finally. "The weather is almost always nice. Even in winter, it's warmer than many other places in Europe. The language is comfortable for me. I can always get what I need. Many of my friends are in and out throughout the year, and there are always plenty of things to do. It's central to the rest of Europe, should I want to be elsewhere. And the atmosphere is more relaxed than in many of the larger cities."

Ben pursed his lips. "Fair enough," he said. "Basically, you like it here." He wondered if he should ask the question at the forefront of his mind.

Léo nodded. "Yes." He arched an eyebrow. "I can almost see you thinking. Ask your questions. If I don't want to answer, I won't."

Ignoring the heat rising yet again in his cheeks, Ben said, "I was just wondering about Malik. He lives here too, right? From how you were talking last night, you guys seem close."

"We are," Léo answered. "My aunt and uncle were persuaded by my mother to send Malik to school in France. There are only five months between our ages, and we were almost inseparable as children. We both have similar life priorities—Malik much prefers Europe to Saudi

Arabia—and so it is not unreasonable that we both enjoy Monaco."

"He's your best friend, isn't he?" Ben asked softly, something in Léo's expression giving away that detail despite his sensible explanation.

Léo merely looked at him. "Come," he said, standing and extending a hand to Ben. "If you have only a few days here, you should be enjoying them."

Ben scrambled out of his chair, wondering exactly what Léo had in mind. His room was just one floor down, although it might take them a while to find it in the rabbit warren of corridors.

They paused briefly at the bar for Léo to take care of the bill—Ben guiltily reached for his own wallet, only to be quelled by Léo's imperiously raised eyebrow—and were soon in the elevator. Ben told himself firmly that he wasn't disappointed when Léo hit the button for the lobby. He'd almost convinced himself of that by the time they made it outside the hotel—and then he experienced another shock when he realized Léo had used the hotel valet parking service.

"Are you nuts?" he hissed. "Do you know how much this costs?" And the valet would need to be tipped too.

"Yes," Léo said, looking faintly surprised that cost would even be a consideration. Ben shut his mouth and reminded himself it wasn't his money. If Léo wanted to spend a ridiculous sum on parking for just— Holy mother of God, was that his *car*?

Ben had never been interested in cars. He had a cousin who'd plastered his walls with car posters as a teen and could tell you to the smallest detail the difference between a... between two similar cars, but for Ben, the only important things were that it ran, it wasn't hideously ugly, and that it didn't cost him more in petrol than his weekly grocery bill.

He didn't think Léo's car got great fuel economy.

His jaw had actually dropped as the valet pulled up in the sports car. It was... well, he wasn't sure, exactly, other than a gleaming, sleek, sexy-looking two-seater that had gained the attention of everyone around.

"This is your car?" he asked faintly. He understood now why Léo would pay for valet parking. No way would he want to park this on the street.

Léo tipped the valet and then gestured toward the car. "Yes. Coming?"

Ben nodded dumbly. The valet opened the door for him, and Ben carefully climbed into the passenger seat. Inside, the car's combination of sleek sportiness and utter luxury was even more apparent. He could smell the leather of his seat, sank into its cushiony comfort. All the finishes were top-notch, and everything was spotless. It was a far cry from the interior of Ben's car, which was usually cluttered with jackets, receipts, and the occasional chocolate bar wrapper.

As Ben considered whether he should try to keep his feet off the floor, just in case his shoes weren't clean enough (and thanked all that was holy that he wasn't wearing his ratty old runners), Léo started the car.

It thrummed.

The purr of the engine and the muted vibration through the seats were... incredible. For the first time, Ben understood why people went nuts for cars. He'd wanted to jump Léo before, but now, his fondest wish was to strip naked and be fucked over the bonnet of this machine.

Although that might end up scratching the paint or something. So maybe not.

"What kind of car is this?" he asked as Léo pulled out of the Fairmont forecourt and onto the road.

"A Bugatti Veyron Grand Sport," Léo told him.

That meant absolutely nothing to Ben. "Oh," he said, trying to sound intelligent. "Is it... new?" He wanted to slap himself for the inane question. "I mean, it's very clean and shiny still. Almost like it hasn't been driven much."

Léo was grinning, an indulgent kind of smile that told Ben he wasn't fooling anyone, but that Léo thought he was cute. "It's nearly eleven years old. I just take very good care of it—it's my favorite car."

As Ben digested the fact that Léo had other cars, and wondered if they were anything like this one, Léo flashed him a broad smile. "So," he said, "it's a gorgeous day. What do you want to see in Monaco?"

Chapter Five

"Are you sure?" Léo asked doubtfully, hesitating outside the building. When he'd lured Ben from the restaurant with the promise of sightseeing—something he detested—he'd thought to take him to some of the exclusive member-only clubs along the marina, or to the private rooms at the casino. Somewhere they could flirt over drinks, slowly ramping up the tension between them as the afternoon whiled away into evening.

Not this.

"Yeah! It'll be fun," Ben enthused, grabbing Léo's hand and dragging him up the steps to... the Musée océanographique. Léo had been visiting Monaco since he was a teenager, and had lived there for years, without ever having entertained the notion of visiting the establishment.

"Fun," Léo repeated. "Aren't you Australian? Why do you want to visit an aquarium when you have the Great Barrier Reef right there?"

Ben dropped his hand. "I don't live anywhere near the Reef, and the last time I got up that way was years ago. I want to see the turtles—I've never seen one in real life before. I guess I can come another time, by myself."

Léo sighed. Despite his bunny's bravado, he could see Ben's disappointment, and as stupid as it made him feel, he wanted to fix it.

"Let's go," he said, trying to muster some enthusiasm as he recaptured Bunny's hand. "Turtles." The way Ben's smile lit his face almost made him forget that he hated places like this. The curve of that mouth….

"Léo?" Ben prompted.

Léo blinked. "I beg your pardon," he said. "What did you say?"

Ben's cheeky grin was ridiculously enticing. "I said, after this, you get to choose what we do next." Bunny flushed bright red, and his gaze darted away. "Anything you want," he finished, his voice a trifle unsteady.

Despite the roaring in his ears, Léo managed a hoarse agreement, already planning what he wanted to do.

It made walking up the steps a little uncomfortable.

The next issue arose quickly when Ben announced his intention to pay for their entry.

"Absolutely not," Léo exclaimed, aghast. "You're a visitor here, and my guest."

The stubborn, mutinous expression Ben had worn last night when Léo had ordered champagne was back, but this time Léo found it less annoying and more… sexy. He wondered briefly if his brains were going soft. Maybe there was a long-hidden strain of insanity in his family?

"You paid for everything last night, and for lunch today," Ben said. "It's my turn. And the next turn is mine too." Léo opened his mouth to protest, and Ben insisted, "I pay. Or we say goodbye now."

He closed his mouth and considered. "I will allow you to pay our admission now," he conceded. "But everything in the future is still open for negotiation." Negotiations that would go his way, he was determined. Generations of business and diplomatic skill were in his blood.

Ben squinted suspiciously at him and looked like he might continue to argue, but the people in the line behind them were growing impatient, so he gave a sharp nod and paid the cashier.

So they could go to the aquarium.

SEVERAL HOURS LATER, Léo led Ben into his home. The apartment was not overly large, certainly smaller than his other homes—far smaller than most—but the location and facilities were second to none.

He dropped his keys onto the original Louis XIV sideboard he'd bought for that express purpose, and gestured toward the living area. "Make yourself comfortable. What would you like—" The sound of running water caught their attention, and they both turned toward the corridor that led to the bathroom.

"Do you have a roommate?" Ben asked, sounding surprised.

"No," Léo said, entirely disgruntled as his plans disintegrated. "It's probably Malik. He has a key."

"Oh." Ben looked disappointed, and Léo couldn't blame him. They'd been subtly teasing each other all afternoon, and Léo was certain that his casual invitation back to his place for drinks hadn't fooled anyone. He wondered how long it would take him to get rid of Malik. The trick would be not seeming too eager for him to go—Malik loved nothing more than to torment him.

There was the sound of a door opening, and moments later his cousin strolled into the living area, his stride hitching only slightly when he saw them. "Well hello. I'm surprised to see you here," he said—in French. Ben sighed and pouted, and Léo resisted the temptation to go over and lick that lip.

"English, please, Malik," he said instead. "Ben doesn't speak French."

"My apologies," Malik said, turning to Ben and inclining his head. "Ben, is it?"

Ben cleared his throat and nodded. "Ben Adams. Nice to meet you."

"And you," Malik said, his smile wicked. "I'm Léo's more intelligent and better-looking cousin, Malik al-Saud."

"I know," Ben said, and then blushed vividly red. "I mean, that you're his cousin, not that you're better-looking. I mean—" He broke off and squeezed his eyes shut as Malik shouted with laughter. Léo hid his own smile, not wanting to add to his bunny's embarrassment. Ben took a deep breath and opened his eyes.

"Glad to meet you, Malik," he said simply, his face still red. Léo decided to intervene before Ben got scared away.

"Let's sit outside," he said, gesturing toward the balcony overlooking the sparkling Mediterranean. As Malik followed Ben, Léo raised an eyebrow. "What are you doing here, Malik?"

Malik shrugged as he settled himself at the café table on the balcony. "I brought your things that you left at the hotel when you didn't come back last night." He didn't leer or put any special emphasis on the words, but Ben's gaze dropped to the tabletop and the color that had begun to die down flared again.

"Well, thank you for that," Léo said, then added, "I came back here. You know I never wanted to stay at the hotel. That was Karim's ridiculous idea."

Ben shot him a grateful look. Léo was not shy when it

came to sex, and the idea that Ben was embarrassed about Malik thinking they'd slept together was a surprising turn-on.

"Did Karim enjoy his visit?" Ben asked Malik politely.

Malik rolled his eyes. "Oh yes. He's having a very good time on his European tour. He said something about maybe passing back through later, but I'm hoping one of his other stops will distract him."

"He's distractible," Léo murmured, his attention on the curve of Ben's neck. He wondered if Ben would let him bite it. "He'll have forgotten all about us and Monaco before he goes to bed tonight."

Ben chuckled, and Malik grinned.

"So, Ben," he said, "how long are you in Monaco?"

"Just another three days," Ben said regretfully. "This was supposed to be like a break from my holiday, because I've been pretty much constantly on the go."

"Where have you been so far?"

As Ben began to recount his journey and Malik asked questions and made comments accordingly, Léo murmured that he would fetch drinks and retreated to the kitchen. Despite the fresh breeze off the water, he felt over-warm. Malik was not malicious or cruel, but he did love to tease, and Léo had honestly expected him to tease Ben. After all, the bunny, with his blushes and stammers and fumbling, was so very teaseable. Instead, his cousin was treating Ben like an old friend.

Léo quickly set up a tray with chilled glasses and sparkling water. He briefly considered wine, or cocktails, but they'd had wine with lunch, and he wanted Ben's head clear—in case Malik learned to read his mind and left soon.

When he returned to the balcony, Ben and Malik were laughing. "You're having me on!" Ben exclaimed, turning his smiling face toward Léo as he set the tray down. "Tell me it's not true," he demanded.

"What is?" Léo asked indulgently, taking a seat and filling a glass for Ben.

"Thank you," Ben said as he took it. "Malik says you got stuck climbing over a fence once," he informed Léo, who immediately shot Malik a dark look.

"It's true," he said reluctantly. "But it wasn't exactly a fence. It was a two-foot-thick nine-foot wall with barbed wire on top." He wondered what other stories Malik had been telling.

Ben blinked. "But...." He looked at Malik. "You said it was the fence around your school."

"It was," Malik said, still grinning. "Léo and I were not the most obedient students. By that time we'd been through several schools, and our parents were reduced to sending us to what was essentially a prison for teenagers."

"Don't exaggerate," Léo told him. "It's one of the top-rated schools in France. Just not as liberal as some of the other schools we went to."

"Léo, they tried to make seventeen-year-old boys go to bed at nine o'clock!"

Léo remembered all the nights he'd huddled under blankets with a flashlight, forced to rely on a book for entertainment for hours until he was tired enough to sleep, and made a face.

"But still," Ben said, "even if it was a nine-foot wall with barbed wire, how did you get stuck for twenty minutes?"

Malik laughed again, and Léo silently vowed to avenge himself. Then a thought occurred and his stomach plummeted. *Please don't—*

"You don't have to take my word for it," Malik said. "There are pictures. The quality isn't great, because it was almost dark and they were taken with a camera phone in 2004, but you can tell it's Léo and the pictures are time stamped."

Ben's face lit up, and need clenched low in Léo's belly. He could handle a bit of humiliation if it put that look on Ben's face. After all, it wasn't as if half of Europe hadn't seen the pictures already.

"Can I see them? Are they here?" Ben was asking eagerly.

"They're online," Malik answered smugly. And well he should be smug, since he was the one who'd posted them, ostensibly to celebrate having been "free" of that school for ten years, but in reality as revenge for Léo telling his then girlfriend that she wasn't worth Malik's time. Léo still maintained he'd done the right thing, especially since the stupid woman had been married and divorced in the two years since, and was engaged again—to a richer and more powerful man than her ex-husband.

Ben had his phone in hand and was asking Malik where to look. Malik also had his phone in hand, sending Ben a friend request on Facebook and tagging him in the post that featured the photos so he could find them more easily. Léo sipped his water and wished it were gin.

Several very long minutes later, after the photos of Léo straddling a cold stone wall with his trousers ripped and yet somehow still caught on the barbed wire had been examined and laughed over, Ben set his phone down on the table and smiled at him.

"I'm so glad you're not perfect," he said guilelessly.

Léo reined back his amusement and lifted an eyebrow. "I'm not?" he asked, while Malik snickered.

"Nope." Ben's answer was cheerful. "I didn't think you were anyway, because you're kind of arrogant, but you were close. Now you're more human, and I like you better that way." He was slightly pink when he finished, and Léo swallowed hard. The silence drew out for long moments, and Léo wondered distantly why Malik was choosing this to be the first moment of his life to be discreetly silent.

"Anyway," Ben mumbled finally. "Can I use your bathroom?"

Good manners sprang to life. "Of course," Léo said. "Down the hall, first door on the left." Ben left them, and Léo sipped again from his glass, his throat suddenly dry.

"That was not what I was expecting at all," Malik said, and Léo met his surprisingly serious gaze.

"What do you mean?"

"Well, to begin with, I thought you'd have fucked him last night and moved on. I was expecting you to come back to the hotel and was already surprised that you'd stayed with him."

"I didn't—"

"I know, and that's even more surprising. Basically, you went on a date with the little bunny."

Léo opened his mouth to protest, but closed it when he realized it was true. He'd wined and dined Ben, then left him chastely in his hotel room after just a few kisses. When was the last time he'd done something like that?

Never.

"And then," Malik continued, "you took him out again today, went to an aquarium, of all places"—Léo winced, realizing he'd left them too much time to talk while he'd been fetching drinks—"and brought him back here. You hardly ever bring men here."

"Well—"

Malik held up a hand. "Not finished. You look at him like he's edible, which doesn't surprise me, but also like he makes your day better. He babbles, and you smile indulgently. It's... surprising. Not bad, really, but surprising."

Léo waited a beat. "Are you done?"

Malik nodded.

"Good. I like him. He's… refreshing. And…." Léo searched for the right word. "Cute," he decided. "He got all upset last night when he found out I don't need a reservation at restaurants."

Malik blinked. "Why?" he asked, bewildered.

Léo shrugged. "No idea. But he was all riled up, and it was adorable. And I hate myself for even using the word adorable, but it's the only one that fits. He's here for a few days, and I enjoy his company, so I'm going to enjoy him while he's here."

Malik looked at him with a carefully blank expression. "Okay," he said finally. "Moving on, Karim asked me if you were gay."

Léo shrugged again. "I thought it might come up after he saw me leaving with Ben. What did you say?"

"I told him you were, and that if he had a problem with it, he needed to keep it to himself. He asked a lot of questions, mostly around what your parents and friends thought. He also asked me three times this morning if you'd be back before he left."

That took Léo aback slightly. "Did he seem angry?"

Malik shook his head. "No. As annoying as the little pest is, you may want to make time to talk with him. It may be that Europe will suit his… temperament… more than Saudi Arabia."

Léo rubbed his forehead. "Uncle wouldn't like it if his son decided to forsake his responsibilities and live in Europe."

"Uncle would like it far less if his son were discovered to be gay," Malik said dryly. "And it's not like Karim is his oldest son."

On the table, Ben's phone dinged and vibrated. Then again. And again. Malik glanced at it, then picked it up.

"Malik!" Léo hissed.

"Who's Dani?" his irrepressible cousin asked.

"His best friend. Put that down!"

"How did lunch go?" Malik read. "'Did you seduce him?' I think Dani deserves bonus points for using 'seduce' in a text message. 'OMG are you having sex right now?' And the last one is really weird. 'I hope he didn't kill you after all.'" Malik glanced at Léo, brows furrowed. "What could Ben have told his friend that would lead her to think you'd kill him?"

"I have no idea," Léo admitted. "She found the Wikipedia page, so she's probably seen some of the tabloid articles too, but I don't think anything in them paints me as a murderer."

Malik shrugged. "Sounds like the friend is a lot like Ben." He put the phone back. "But in case you were worried about whether you were going to get him into bed, it seems like he's a pretty certain bet."

"Thanks," Léo said dryly.

Ben rejoined them, and Léo had a moment of utter relief that they hadn't been caught invading his privacy. He might have to find a way to subtly suggest Ben change his phone settings so the contents of text messages weren't displayed on the lock screen. Léo had done that years ago, as his family couldn't be trusted not to look.

Gabriel had once gotten quite an education by being nosy.

"Your phone beeped a few times," Malik said helpfully.

Ben smiled and picked it up as he sat down. "Thank you." He glanced at it and blanched. Malik watched, smirking, as Ben swiped the screen. "Excuse me," he muttered. "It's Dani. I just have to—" He tapped away for a few moments before slipping the phone into his pocket. "Sorry about that."

"Is your friend also here?" Malik asked.

Ben shook his head. "No, she's at home in Australia. She just likes to know everything I'm doing."

Malik frowned. "Isn't it quite late in Australia?" He looked at his watch. "I can never keep all the time zones straight, but I'm certain that early evening here means wee hours of the morning there."

Ben winced. "Yeah. It's about two in the morning, I think. She's, uh, she stayed up because she wanted... she wanted to hear about my visit to the Musée océanographique."

Léo couldn't hold back his smile, and he doubted Malik even tried. "She's a marine fan, then?" his cousin teased.

Ben studiously looked out at the water. "Yeah. She, uh, loves the ocean."

Léo took pity on his bunny and changed the subject. "We haven't yet talked about your plans while you're here."

Ben seized on the lifeline and began to chatter about visiting the Prince's Palace, wandering through the streets and "soaking up atmosphere"—Léo and Malik exchanged bewildered glances at that—and possible jaunts to Nice. Malik helpfully suggested some areas in the countryside surrounding Monaco that might be of interest—Léo recognized all of them as places Malik had taken women for "romantic" dates—but Léo could tell from his cousin's expression that he was plotting something.

"So, Ben," he finally said, and Léo kicked him under the table. It mustn't have been hard enough, because he was ignored. "I couldn't help but glance at your phone when it went off before—my apologies—and I noticed something that made me curious."

Ben's eyes widened. "Er...."

"What did your friend mean when she said she hoped Léo hadn't killed you?"

Relief crossed Ben's face, followed closely by mortification. "Um... that was just a silly joke," he said weakly.

Malik cocked his head. "Really? I don't get it." He smiled charmingly. Léo could actually see Ben relax in the face of that smile. He'd always wondered how his cousin did that. He picked up his glass, wondering once again if it was something that could be learned.

"Well, it's like.... You know those movies, where some random, ordinary person sees something that turns out to be highly classified? And then a government assassin is sent to silence them?"

Léo choked on his water, and Malik's jaw dropped.

"You... thought Léo was a government assassin sent to kill you?"

Ben screwed up his face. "It sounds stupid when you say it like that."

"Really?" Léo asked incredulously. "Only when he says it like that?" He looked down at his clothing, wondering what about his custom-tailored designer apparel said "government flunky" and "murderer." He looked back at Ben, and his dick surged to life at the sight of Bunny chewing on his lower lip.

"I know it's silly," Ben admitted. "But it seemed to make a lot of sense when I was talking to Dani this morning. Well, kind of."

"How exactly did that conversation go?" Malik asked curiously.

Ben flushed and shook his head. "Look, it was stupid. I

was telling her about last night, and she said it sounded kind of like a movie."

Léo found himself utterly befuddled yet again. It seemed to be a common thing when he was speaking with Ben, and he wasn't sure he liked it. He ran the events of the previous evening through his mind and came up blank.

"What the heck did you two do last night that sounded like a movie where the government assassinates someone?" Malik demanded, his gaze on Léo, who just shrugged.

"No, that's not...." Ben trailed off helplessly. "Léo, you explain it."

Léo stared at him, astonished. "You want me to explain it?"

Ben nodded.

Léo shook his head. "What, exactly, am I explaining?"

The sigh Ben gave contained the weight of the world. "I guess you don't see it, but try to be me." He cast a doubtful glance at Léo. "Okay, that may not be within the scope of the possible. Just.... So I'm in the casino, and this incredibly hot guy approaches me. He turns out to not only be gorgeous, but also really nice and incredibly wealthy and the son of a princess, for God's sake."

Léo shifted, a little uncomfortable. He'd always been aware that fate had been kind to him, but hearing it all itemized was... unsettling.

"And then not only does this—this Adonis deign to speak to me, he buys me incredible champagne and takes me to dinner at a fully booked restaurant and we have drinks overlooking the ocean in a casino that is considered one of the bywords for glamour in the modern world. Things like that don't happen to normal people. So when Dani said it sounded like a movie...."

"You immediately thought of the kind that didn't end

well for the 'normal' person," Malik said understandingly. Ben nodded. "That's not very flattering to you, Ben."

Ben shrugged. "The odds all point in that direction."

Léo leaned forward, hooked a hand around Ben's nape, and pulled him forward into a kiss. Finally, finally, after hours of waiting and flirting and looking at turtles, he sucked on that lip, licking into Ben's warm, delicious mouth.

Distantly, he heard Malik excusing himself, and then the sound of the front door slamming. When Léo eventually drew back, they were both breathless and Ben's eyes were glassy.

"You are not a 'normal' person," Léo whispered.

Ben's expression changed from dreamy to hurt, and he pulled away. Léo watched, bewildered, as he got up and began gathering the glasses from the table.

"Ben?"

"Yeah, uh, just... I'll call a cab or something. Or I bet it's not too far to walk back to my hotel from here. I mean, nothing's really far in Monaco, right? Ha ha."

"You're leaving?" Léo was shocked. Why was he going? After their day together, and that kiss.... Also, Dani's message had all but said outright that Ben had been planning to have sex with him. "Ben, put that down. What's wrong?"

Ben set the tray back on the table, took a deep breath, and looked Léo in the eye. "I know I'm a bit... well, odd sometimes. I know I talk a lot and make some weird leaps of logic. And I know I'm really nothing like you and your friends. But it kind of stings to be kissed like that and then told I'm not normal."

Léo blinked, then started to laugh. He couldn't even blame it on a language barrier, just a stupid miscommunication. Ben made a hurt sound and spun around, and Léo lunged out of his chair to grab his bunny's hand.

"Wait, please. I apologize, I shouldn't be laughing. It's just... we are talking at cross-purposes." Bunny wouldn't meet his eyes. His face was flushed, and his lower lip trembled slightly. Léo couldn't resist; he bent and dropped a kiss on that mouth. "When I said you weren't normal, I meant in the sense we were talking about before. You said that wonderful, exciting, 'fairy-tale' things didn't happen to 'normal' people. You're not one of those people, Ben. You're extraordinary. You're worthy of a Hollywood movie plot, and before you start thinking about assassination and bets and whatever else, I mean that in the best way."

Ben looked at him skeptically. "Before you lay it on too thick, you should probably know that as long as you're not calling me a freak, I'm pretty much a sure thing."

As hard as he tried, Léo couldn't hold back his laughter. He pulled Ben into his arms and kissed him again, reveling in the warm, soft lips against his, the startled mewl that Ben made. This time he got his tongue in on the action. His bunny tasted delicious, and felt incredible against him, all lean, firm muscle and limbs, and soft skin, and a thrilling shiver ran down Léo's spine. His belly clenched in arousal, and he reluctantly drew back.

"Sure thing or not, you're... amazing. You make me laugh. You show me things from a different perspective, even if I don't understand it. You got me to willingly enter an aquarium and spend hours there."

"You loved it!" Ben cried indignantly. While Léo was willing to concede it hadn't been as bad as he'd imagined, he wouldn't say he'd loved it, so he just smiled and kissed Ben again. It wasn't a quick kiss, and by the time they pulled apart for air, they were both hard and wanting.

"Bed?" Ben whispered. "Or a couch? Or... somewhere

that's not on this balcony, because I don't want to trauma-
tize any seagulls."

Caught between laughter and wanting to just bend
Ben over the table and damn the seagulls, Léo opted for
sanity and dragged Ben inside. Unfortunately, this was
his bunny, and although Léo didn't see it happen, he
later assumed that the combination of desire and Léo
rushing him and just his being Ben meant that he
tripped.

Ben made a sound between a yelp and a cry a split
second before he slammed into Léo, sending them both
tumbling through the thankfully open door and to the floor
in the living room. They skidded a few feet across the
polished hardwood floor and ended up sprawled in a
tangle of limbs.

Ben made a distressed sound. Léo stared at the ceiling,
wondering what had just happened.

"You knocked me off my feet," he said. It was literally
true, but, thinking back on the events of the last day, it was
metaphorically true as well.

"I'm sorry!" Ben cried. He wriggled, trying to disen-
tangle himself. "I'm such a nong, I'm so sorry."

Léo grabbed a flailing arm and hauled Ben closer.
"Stop. You're not a… nong." Whatever that was. "All is
well. I shouldn't have yanked at you like that." He chuckled. "But if you think about it, this all fits with what I was
saying before about you being extraordinary. You knocked
me off my feet."

There was a moment of silence, then Ben shouted with
laughter. "Oh my God, you did not just say that!" He wriggled again, but this time he wasn't trying to get away.
Instead, he climbed on top of Léo and kissed him.

Within moments, Léo had his hands inside Ben's shirt,
stroking the warm, soft skin of his back. Lean muscles

flexed under his hands, and he tore his mouth away from Ben's to explore the rougher skin of his neck.

"Shirt off," he murmured, nibbling an earlobe, and Ben made a sound of agreement.

Shirts came off, and shoes, and then trousers. Léo couldn't tear his eyes—or hands—away from Ben. With clothes on, he was almost gawky, but without them the fitness of his slender frame was more apparent. Léo loved the lithe line of his body, the contrast of his paler skin against Léo's own, the little shiver he gave as Léo circled his nipple with a forefinger. Léo replaced his digit with his mouth, and Ben moaned, his nipple a hard button under Léo's tongue.

"Léo," he gasped. "This whole day has been foreplay. Consider me an easy lay. Condoms?"

Léo thought maybe he was supposed to laugh, but he was too busy licking down Ben's stomach. A hand in his hair wrenched his head back, and he blinked at his bunny's determined face.

"Léo! Condoms and lube. Where?"

"Bedroom," Léo said dazedly, and Ben let go of his hair and scrambled up off the floor, both completely graceless and strangely graceful. He hurried toward the hallway, clad only in his underwear, and Léo watched him go, admiring the way his arse moved under the black fabric. That arse disappeared around the corner with the rest of Ben, and Léo realized that not only did he definitely want to follow, but that his apartment had four bedrooms and since the master was at the end of the hall, Ben would probably appreciate some direction.

He rose and strode after his nimble—*nubile*—bunny, finding him reaching for the door of the room Léo used as an office. "Keep going," he said, his voice a little husky.

Ben turned and kept walking down the hall, shooting Léo a look over his shoulder. "Where?"

"Last door." Léo caught up quickly, reaching out to touch, to stroke… to squeeze. Ben moaned, hesitated, and Léo urged him on, hand on his arse. Just a few steps more… then they were in Léo's bedroom, and he was stripping off Ben's underwear, his hand on bare, naked, warm skin, Ben's hard, pulsing dick rubbing against him. Somehow they made it to the bed. Ben's hands were in Léo's briefs, then the briefs were gone and Ben was dropping to his knees, and *oh*, it was so good, hot, wet…. Ben's mouth was a miracle, but he wanted in that arse.

"Stop," he panted. "I want to fuck you."

Ben pulled back, lips shiny, and smiled. He scrambled to his feet, turned, and bent over the bed, peering back over his shoulder. "I want that too."

Léo fumbled in the nightstand for lube, then cursed. "Wait." He strode across to the en suite bath to find condoms. He rarely invited hookups to his home, so there was no need to keep them by the bed.

He found them and rushed back to the bedroom. Ben had moved, was lying on his back across the mattress, knees drawn up, stretching himself, and the very sight sent all the blood in Léo's head rushing to his cock. He gulped.

"You look amazing," he said hoarsely.

Ben turned his head and smiled at him, and that was all Léo needed.

Within moments he was on the bed, stretching over his lithe, beautiful, *sexy* bunny, kissing him, worshipping his mouth, and then the condom was on and he pressed inside Ben's hot, tight arse.

They both groaned.

Slowly, slowly, Léo inched in, a vise grip on his control. He pulled back, slid forward again, repeating the action several times until Ben grabbed his shoulders, fingers digging in, and demanded, "Fuck me, please!"

So Léo did.

He drew back and then surged, thrusting hard enough to make Ben cry out. For a moment he hesitated, but Ben yelled, "Don't stop, idiot!" and that spurred him on. Nothing had ever felt as good as this, Ben's body around him, Ben garbling nonsense phrases interspersed with shouts of "Yes, there!" and "Oh God, harder!" that made him feel invincible and desperate at the same time.

Sweat ran down his body as Ben came, clenching tight around his dick, and he was unable to hold on anymore.

By the time his brain came back online and he realized he was collapsed on top of Ben, their breathing had had time to settle. Ben was stroking him, a hand rubbing over his back. It was nice.

"Am I too heavy?" he mumbled. He wasn't quite ready to move, but he didn't want Ben to be uncomfortable.

"No, I like it." His bunny sounded thoughtful. "I kind of regret that I made us go see the turtles, though. We could have been doing this all afternoon."

Léo barely dredged up the energy to laugh.

Chapter Six

B en woke slowly, feeling wonderful. The pillow under
his head was the perfect density, and the arm slung
over his waist—

Léo.

His eyes snapped open. He'd had sex with Léo. And
not just any sex, not garden-variety sex that was good and
satisfying but easily done. No, he'd had hot, screaming,
nerve-wrenching, life-changing sex. Twice. And then again
just before dawn when he'd accidentally woken Léo by
tripping on his own feet on his way back from the en suite
bathroom.

Three times.

In one night.

And he felt *awesome*.

Well, maybe a little tender, but in the best possible way.

Ben wriggled back a little so that his body was in full
contact with Léo's. For a dilettante playboy who didn't
work and ate and drank exceptionally rich food and wine,
the man was in excellent shape. Nude, he looked like he
should be in a men's health magazine, and Ben loved the

sensation of all that firm, rippled muscle against him now. He wriggled again, just because he could.

Léo chuckled.

Ben jumped and tried to jerk away, but the arm around him tightened, fitting them so close together that a tissue wouldn't have fit between them. And either Léo had stashed a torch in the bed, or he was very happy to have Ben snuggled against him.

Ben's dick perked up at the thought.

"Good morning," Léo murmured in his ear, his voice husky and growly, and Ben shivered.

"Hi," he said lamely. "Um, I mean good morning. Did you sleep well?"

Léo stretched, and Ben grinned foolishly as muscles shifted against his skin. "I slept very well. What time is it?"

Squinting at his watch in the dimly lit room, Ben said, "A little after nine. Wow, we slept late."

Léo chuckled again. "Well, we were worn out." He sat up, pulling a protesting Ben with him, and threw back the covers.

Ben pouted. "I was all warm and comfy," he complained. "I'm on holiday in Monaco. I'm supposed to do things like sleep late."

Léo kissed him, quickly at first, but then came back for a long, lingering kiss that heated rapidly and made Ben so hard his dick could have pounded nails. He wrapped his arms around Léo, but just as he was seriously thinking about round four (four times in less than a day!), Léo pulled back.

"Léo," Ben whined, and Léo dropped another quick kiss on his mouth, pausing to gently bite Ben's lower lip.

"Up," Léo said firmly. "You're on holiday in Monaco. You should see everything that makes this place what it is." He disentangled himself from Ben and got up, strolling naked to the windows to open the curtains. Ben was admiring the view when glaringly bright sunshine flooded in, blinding him. By the time he was finally able to see again, Léo had left the room.

Scowling, Ben clambered toward the edge of the king-size bed, but somehow he got caught in the covers and ended up pitching off face-first, thankfully catching himself before his nose made contact with the floor. The rug was plush, but he didn't think it would blunt the impact completely.

Glad that Léo hadn't seen his less-than-graceful dismount, he scrambled to his feet and spent a moment wondering what he should do next. Get dressed? Should he help himself to the shower? Or wander out naked to see what Léo was doing? He'd had one-night stands before, but this wasn't exactly that... or was it? Was Léo expecting him to discreetly bug off?

"I can almost see the gears turning in your head," Léo's amused voice said, and Ben swung around to see him standing in the doorway—still naked.

"Uh... what do you mean?" Ben stalled, wondering if he should just straight-out ask.

"You were thinking very hard. What has your brain so busy?"

Crap. I'm not sure if you're done with me and I'm overstaying my welcome. No way was he saying that. "Um. I was... I need coffee." He seized on the excuse.

Léo smiled. "It should be ready soon. And then I thought we'd go to the club for brunch."

Ben froze even as something inside him did a happy dance. Léo didn't want to get rid of him after all, but oh my God, the *club*? Did he mean the yacht club? What the fuck was Ben going to do at the yacht club?

"The club?" he asked carefully. "The yacht club you

mentioned yesterday?" Léo nodded, and Ben nodded, but then he stopped because the nod felt a little too enthusiastic, like maybe he'd turned into a bobblehead doll. "I, um, I should...." Léo's face became a carefully neutral mask, and Ben hesitated. Why shouldn't he go to the yacht club? He'd likely never again get the chance to see the inside of an exclusive members-only yacht club in Monaco. He had the wardrobe for it now. And Léo would be there to show him the ropes, so it wasn't like he could make too big an arse of himself.

Ben carefully didn't think about all the ways he could make an arse of himself.

"I should probably go back to my hotel and change," he said. "But coffee first."

Léo smiled.

BEN SLIPPED INTO THE TAXI. "The Fairmont, please," he told the driver, and pulled out his phone. He was pretty sure it wouldn't take long to get there, since nothing in Monaco was far away, but if he didn't check in with Dani, she'd start planning his assassination.

As the phone rang in his ear, he grinned. Assassination. Hadn't Léo and Malik been surprised when they'd heard that theory?

"Finally!" Dani shrieked in his ear, and Ben winced and pulled the phone away as the driver glanced back over his shoulder.

"Hey, Dani," he said weakly.

"Don't you 'hey' me! I got one lousy text more than twelve hours ago saying 'all good, talk later,' and then nothing!"

"Well, I was kinda busy," Ben defended.

She went silent, and he wasn't sure if that was a sign of acceptance or uncontrollable rage. "Busy… like carnally?"

Ben rolled his eyes. "Oh my God, Dani."

"Well?" she insisted, and he gave in.

"Yes."

She cheered. Actually cheered.

Ben rolled his eyes again.

"I know you're rolling your eyes," she said.

"Good, then I don't need to tell you you're an idiot."

"No, but you do need to tell me what happened. Not the details," she tacked on hastily. "Just a vague outline."

Ben sighed and slumped back against the seat. "A vague outline? Okay."

"Really?" Her surprise was evident, and he had to grin.

"Yes, really. So, vaguely, we met for lunch." He was glad that vague meant he didn't have to tell her about the debacle in the lobby of the Fairmont.

Well, not yet, anyway.

"After lunch—oh my God, I nearly forgot. His car, Dani!"

"His *car*?" Dani sounded confused. "Is that a euphemism?"

Ben snorted. "No, you loser. I'm talking about his actual car."

"Since when do you care anything about cars?" The skepticism in Dani's voice was heavy.

"Since I've been in this one. It was a religious experience, I'm not joking." Ben closed his eyes and remembered riding in the magnificent machine, which was to ordinary cars as the glorious champagne of the other evening was to the plonk he usually drank.

"A religious experience. Right. What was it, a Porsche or something?"

"Not a Porsche," Ben said. "A Bugatti Veyron Grand

Sport." He still really had no idea what that meant, but figured Dani would already be looking it up, and she could tell him all about it. Sure enough, that was the sound of her keyboard clicking away....

"Wow!"

"Yep," Ben said smugly. "Léo's is an older one, nearly eleven years old, but it's pretty amazing."

Dani laughed. "Benji, you moron, this isn't like a Ford where they release a new model every year. It doesn't matter how old Léo's is, it won't devalue. This is a limited edition car—there were only four hundred and fifty Veyrons ever made, and they're completely sold out."

Ben was even more glad that he hadn't been wearing his grotty old shoes. "Are you reading that off the website?" he asked, in an attempt to avoid saying anything stupid.

"Pretty much. Also, whatever you do, don't look up the cost of this car."

"That bad?" Ben winced.

"You'll be scared to walk too close to it," she confirmed. He remembered again how it had felt to ride in that car, and even though she couldn't see him, he shook his head.

"Dani, it's a risk I'm willing to take."

She laughed again. "Okay, so back to the vague outline. What happened after lunch?"

"We went to the Musée océanographique, then back to his place for drinks. That's where I was when you texted. Malik was there for a while, then he left and Léo and I—" He hesitated, glancing at the driver. "We got to know each other better." As soon as he said it, he wished he hadn't. As a euphemism, it wasn't very vague.

"Okay," Dani mused. "Vague outlines suck balls. Give me details about everything up until clothes came off. And then tell me about this morning. After clothes went back on."

The cab pulled into the Fairmont's drive and under the portico. "Hold on," Ben told Dani, and leaned forward to pay the driver. Once he was walking into the hotel, he put the phone back to his ear. "Sorry. Okay, details." As he crossed the large lobby toward the elevators that led to his part of the hotel, he recounted what had happened at lunch and the aquarium in a little more detail. By the time he finished telling her about Léo's alternately (adorably) whiny and fascinated attitude at the Musée océanographique, he was stepping out of the elevator on his floor.

"So then back to his place for drinks?" Dani said as he checked the signs and walked down one of the several seemingly identical corridors. The problem with hotels that weren't built in standard shapes was that they were way too easy to get lost in.

"Yep, back to his place for drinks. Malik was there when—"

"Wait, tell me about his place first, before I get distracted," she insisted.

He sighed, but mostly for effect. Léo's apartment was pretty spectacular. "Well, to start with, it's bigger than your place and mine combined. I mean, I know neither of us live in big places, but still, considering what the price of property is supposed to be like here, it's a big space for one person. Overlooking the ocean, gorgeous balcony the size of my bedroom. Solid timber furniture, and I think some of it was antique. And, Dani, God, the *bathroom*! I could move into it."

"Ocean view, you say?" she said, seemingly stuck on that.

"Yes," he answered as he stopped in front of his door

and fumbled in his pocket for the key card. "From the living area *and* the master bedroom. But that's not entirely rare here, Dani. Practically the entire place is built on a hill rising from the sea." He pushed into the room and tossed the card on the desk as the door closed behind him. His room was reassuringly exactly as he had left it, with his new clothes strewn everywhere.

"Do you know where it is?"

Ben kicked off his boat shoes, which had been surprisingly comfortable, damn it, and flopped on the bed. "I wasn't really paying that much attention to street signs, Dani," he said. "And I didn't ask for his addy."

"Come on," she wheedled. "You must have seen something. How far from the marina was it?"

"Wait," he said, squinting at the ceiling. "As we drove into the garage, there was a sign. It might have been the name of the building."

"What was it?" she demanded.

He heard tapping and clicking, presumably as she prepared to type whatever he told her into Google.

"Like I could pronounce it," he scoffed, and she heaved a sigh.

"So spell it, then." He pulled the phone away from his ear and glared at it. When he put it back, she said, "Making faces at me is not going to change anything."

He growled a little, then forwent comment and spelled out what he could remember from the sign. She tapped away, then said, "Got it!"

A moment later that was followed by "Fuck me!" and Ben groaned. Not again.

"What now?" he asked, rolling over and pressing his face into the pillow. Unfortunately, that muffled Dani's voice, so he pulled it out again.

"...but aside from the fabulous neighbors, do you know

what it means to have property on Avenue Princesse Grace?"

"What does it mean?" Ben was totally resigned to the answer. He was. Really.

"Let's just say, if your dinky eight-square unit was there, based on location alone, it would be worth over ten million Aussie dollars."

Ben sat up. "Say what?" He'd walked on the floors with his shoes on! He'd peed in the toilet!

Dani's laugh made him realize he'd said that out loud.

"I'm hanging up now," he said.

"No, don't! I'll be good, I promise," Dani pleaded. He lay back down and sighed. "That was a big sigh," she prompted.

"Yeah. It's stupid. Just…. Léo's so nice. And hot. And he likes me. That's weird, right? Billionaires aren't supposed to like people like me."

"You're too hard on yourself. Most people like you, so why wouldn't billionaires?"

"That's the dumbest thing I've ever heard," Ben told her, putting his arm over his eyes.

"Dumber than 'I peed in the toilet'?"

He snorted. "I was in shock. Can't be held accountable."

"Right." She sounded skeptical. "So, Léo is hot and nice and likes you, and this depresses you? I gotta tell you, Benji, there are a lot of people who would have you committed for this."

"Don't call me Benji," he said automatically. "And it's not Léo that depresses me. Well, not exactly. It's just… he was so awesome yesterday, and last night was amazing, and even though I decided this was going to be a fairy-tale fling, maybe part of me started thinking how great every-thing is. And how it would be really great to spend more time with Léo. Which is stupid, because it's been less than forty-eight hours since I met him, right? And this was only supposed to be a fling. And the cost of his bathroom could pay for my entire apartment and then some, not to mention his neighbors are… who did you say?"

"Never mind," Dani said. "Better that you not know. But, hon, this is not that big a deal. From the sounds of it, the money kind of slips into second place when you're around Léo, right?"

"Yeah," Ben admitted. "I mean, you can't ignore it, because it's part of everything about him. His clothes, his car, the places he eats and what he orders, all of it. But he's so interesting and cool that he kind of takes over."

"Okay, so focus on that, on Léo. You've got, what, nearly three days left there? Spend that time with him. Maybe the two of you will get sick of each other. Maybe he'll do something really douchey. Then you can leave with a great experience under your belt and no regrets. Or, maybe he'll still be awesome and you'll want to spend more time with him, so you tweak your travel plans and extend your stay. You're not on a schedule, Ben, remember?"

"Yeah…," Ben said slowly, then cheered up. "Yes. I can spend the next couple days as planned, and then if things are good, and I want to, I'll just stay a couple more days."

"Or weeks," Dani suggested. He ignored that. "So what's the plan for today?"

Ben glanced at his watch and leaped off the bed. "The plan is for me to move my arse because I'm going to be late. Léo and I are going for brunch at the yacht club."

There was silence down the line, and Ben grinned smugly as he headed for the bathroom. "Shocked silent, are you?"

"The *yacht club*?" Dani practically screeched. "Oh my God, does he have a *yacht*?"

Ben paused in adjusting the shower temperature. "I don't know. I didn't ask."

"You should. And then text me the answer. And find out which yacht club. And I haven't forgotten that we didn't talk about Malik. I read his Wikipedia page too, so I have questions."

"He was nice. Funny. Not as intense as Léo," Ben said, dropping his pants and stretching. Then he remembered how much the pants had cost, picked them up off the floor, and went to lay them neatly on the bed. He took his shirt off while he was there. "Okay, Dani, I need to shower, but I'll call you later... well, maybe tomorrow. We'll see."

"Text me so I know you're okay," she said, and he felt a rush of affection.

"I will. Love you." He ended the call on her kissy noises and went to shower.

Another day with Léo awaited.

Chapter Seven

B en thought he was handling the yacht club pretty well. He hadn't tripped, walked into anything, dropped anything, or said anything stupid since they'd arrived half an hour ago. Léo had given him a brief tour of the facilities—and oh my God, he'd had no idea rich people actually lived like this—before they'd settled at a table overlooking the marina and ordered brunch. And drinks, because apparently it was expected to drink alcohol with breakfast on a weekday when you were at a private club in Monaco.

Who knew?

Ben tried to ignore that tiny niggling voice at the back of his mind that kept reminding him *he* was on vacation, but Léo did this *all the time* because he *didn't work*. Every time Ben thought about not working, he remembered the long days of summer holidays as a kid, when the initial couple of weeks had been awesome but then the boredom had set in.

Taking a deep breath, Ben looked around. The restaurant was elegant and expensive-looking, yet somehow still casual, and the view over the marina was spectacular. He was on holiday and had a gorgeous, sexy, *nice* guy to keep him company.

Could he really ask for more?

"Léo!" A tall, gorgeous blond man with the same presence as Léo came up to their table, grinning widely. Léo sighed.

"Lucien," he said in a resigned voice. "What are you doing here?"

"The same thing as you, I imagine," Blondie said. "In fact, I'll join you, will I? You must be Ben. Lucien Morel," he continued, and Ben realized with a start that the man had been speaking in English all along, albeit with a heavier French accent than either Léo or Malik. He looked at the man—Lucien—more closely. He was pretty sure he'd been one of the men with Léo in the Place du Casino the other night, one of the ones who didn't go into the casino.

Maybe.

But how did he know Ben's name?

Lucien hesitated midway through grabbing a chair from another table. "We should probably move to a bigger table," he suggested. "The three of us might just be able to squeeze in here, but it will be uncomfortable when Malik arrives."

Léo closed his eyes as Ben turned a bewildered gaze on him. "Malik's coming?" he asked.

"Why is Malik coming?" Léo asked Lucien in a long-suffering tone. Lucien looked around, and as if by magic a staff member appeared. Lucien rattled something off in French, and the man immediately began bustling around to move them to the next table over, which was set for four.

"Malik's coming because I called him," Lucien told Léo, and went to slide into the chair the waiter was holding. Léo groaned, then met Ben's gaze.

"I can make them leave us alone," he said. "They'll still sit right there"—he jerked his head toward Lucien—"and watch us, but they won't talk to us."

Ben laughed. He just couldn't help it. Léo's friends sounded kind of like Dani. "Nah," he said. "It'll be fine."

Léo sighed again, then got up and held out a hand. "Come on, then," he said, sounding like they were off to face a firing squad.

Ben took his hand, and in moments they were settled again at the new table, the waiter having ferried their drinks across for them.

"You've ordered, yes?" Lucien asked, his attention on the menu in his hands. Léo just glared at him, so Ben said, "Yes," and Lucien nodded. He gave his order to the waiter, hesitated, then called the man back and ordered for Malik as well.

"Otherwise he steals off everyone's plates," he told Ben. "He has no patience. He always orders the same thing here, anyway."

Ben bit his lip to stifle a laugh.

"So!" Lucien sat back. "You're Léo's little bunny."

Ben blinked. *What?*

"There's Malik," Léo said, an edge to his tone that made Ben look at him in surprise, but Léo's attention was focused on his cousin as Malik crossed the room toward them. He slid into the last empty chair and grinned at Léo.

"Romantic brunch at the club?"

"Not anymore," Léo grumbled.

Malik laughed. "It's better that we're here to talk you up to Ben, anyway," he said, winking at Ben, who felt his cheeks getting hot.

"Ooh, he blushes!" Lucien exclaimed, and then jumped. Based on the glare he sent at Léo, Ben guessed Léo had just kicked him. He reached over and put his hand on Léo's thigh, because gallantry like that deserved a reward. Léo laid a hand on his, but continued to glare at his friend.

"Lucien," Ben said, in an attempt to distract them all, "do you live here in Monaco too?"

Lucien tore his gaze away from Léo's and smiled at Ben, his blue eyes dancing once more. "No," he said. "Not all the time. I live in Paris, but I visit here often. After all, two of my dearest friends live here."

"Lucien went to school with Léo and me," Malik told Ben. "Well, for a year or so, anyway. Where's the waiter? I need a menu." He looked around.

"No, you don't," Lucien said. "I ordered for you."

Malik frowned. "What did you do that for?" he demanded. "How could you possibly know what I wanted to eat?"

Léo snorted. "Please, Malik. Even if Lucien hadn't ordered for you, you wouldn't have needed the menu. Every time we have breakfast here, you get the same thing."

"I do not!"

Lucien laughed, and Léo raised an eyebrow. Malik pouted, and it was so different from his usually arrogant expression that Ben wanted to hug him. "Well, maybe this time I wanted something different," he protested.

Two waiters approached the table and set their food down. Malik looked at his plate and sighed. "I hate when you're right," he said, and picked up his fork. Ben grinned at his own delicious-looking food, but when he tried to move his hand from Léo's leg, he found it firmly caught in the other man's grip. He turned to look at Léo, but Léo was forking up his quiche, his attention seemingly split between his plate and the good-natured bickering still going on between Malik and Lucien. Ben tugged lightly at his hand, but Léo was definitely not letting go, even as he pretended nothing was happening.

"Is everything all right, Ben?" Malik asked, and Ben started, whipping his head around to look across the table. His cheeks got hot.

"Yes, fine." He grabbed his fork, thankful that he didn't actually need both hands to eat his crepes.

"So," Lucien said, "Malik tells me you've been traveling through Europe. Where's your next stop?"

Ben swallowed a bite. "Italy," he said. "I'm starting in Milan, then working my way south down the west side to Sicily. I'll come back up to Venice, and then after that I'm headed to Switzerland."

Lucien tipped his head to the side and studied Ben. "I don't know you well—"

"Or at all," Léo interrupted dryly, and Malik chuckled.

"—but I think you'll like Venice best."

"Why's that?" Ben asked, fascinated by this almost serious side of a man who'd seemed to be constant merriment.

"It's both ridiculously fanciful and extremely practical. You'll see," he promised, and then grinned, the cheeky side back. "It's also best visited in company. You should meet him there," he said to Léo.

Yes! something in Ben cried, and he was really glad Léo had discouraged Lucien from commenting on his blushes, because he was pretty sure his face was lobster red. "I'm sure Léo's been before," he muttered. "Anyway, you went to school with these two? Was that before or after they stole the headmaster's car to go and buy cigarettes?"

"Oh, before," Lucien said immediately, smiling, although he had a curious expression on his face. "I was with them for that."

"I meant to ask yesterday, but forgot," Ben went on, feeling as though Léo's gaze was burning into the side of his face, "do any of you still smoke?"

Malik shouted with laughter, and Ben blinked. It seemed an extreme reaction to the question.

Lucien shook his head. "None of us smoked then," he said. "It was more by way of a...." He frowned and said something to Léo in French.

"A prank," Léo supplied. Ben turned to look at him, glad that the heat in his cheeks had subsided. "Buying cigarettes, which were strictly forbidden at that school, was just a way of making sure everyone knew we had taken the car." He squeezed Ben's hand, and warmth flowed into Ben's chest. It felt so good to sit there holding Léo's hand.

He was pretty sure he'd be staying in Monaco a bit longer than planned. All he had to do was find a way to broach that with Léo without sounding like a clingy, romantic sap. After all, they'd known each other less than forty-eight hours.

Almost as though he'd read Ben's mind, Lucien asked, "When do you go to Italy?"

Ben hesitated and wished he could fight off the heat creeping up from his collar. "Well," he began, "I'm supposed to leave in two days. But nothing's really set in stone. Dani and I put together an itinerary, but didn't actually book anything, just in case I changed my mind about where I wanted to go or how long I wanted to stay." There, that was sufficiently vague. It told them what his plans were while making it clear he was open to staying longer. Right?

"Only two more days?" Lucien said, shooting a glance

at Léo. "You should stay longer than that. Malik said you've been traveling for a while. You need some time to relax. Another week, at least. Don't you think?" He turned to Malik, hands spread wide, and Malik agreed enthusiastically. Ben couldn't help but notice that Léo remained silent.

"So you're staying, then," Lucien announced. "Did you have plans for today? We should go out on the water."

"Um…." Ben carefully avoided looking at Léo. He didn't want to seem clingy, but since meeting Léo, the sum total of his plans in Monaco was to spend time with him.

"The water is a good idea," Léo declared. He squeezed Ben's hand again. "Part of experiencing life in Monaco," he told him, and Ben smiled and nodded, his heart clenching helplessly.

Two hours later, propped on a sun lounger on the upper deck (because of course there was more than one deck) of Malik's yacht, with a martini in his hand and a hot billionaire beside him, Ben decided that he could probably get used to this life. The sun was shining—not too hot, but deliciously warm—and Malik's yacht came equipped with not just a captain, but also two stewards to serve their every whim. Snacks and drinks had been in constant supply. The ocean sparkled as they cruised along, the color impossibly blue, and Ben sipped from his glass.

"Having fun?" Léo asked lazily, and Ben turned his head to smile at him.

"Oh yeah. You were right, this is definitely a new experience I didn't want to miss."

"I should think not," Lucien said, coming out on the

deck and dropping into a chair a few feet away. "Where's Malik?"

Léo waved a hand toward where Malik was propped against the railing, talking on the phone. "One of his women called. I think he's been trying to shake her off lately, but you know Malik. He can't be rude to a woman."

Ben wasn't sure whether to be aghast that Malik apparently had multiple women that he "shook off," or reassured that he couldn't be rude to women. In the end, he decided that since he wasn't a woman and thus wasn't affected by either circumstance, he didn't care. He took another sip of his martini and wondered whether that was helping him to not care.

Malik ended his call and joined them, and a moment later one of the stewards appeared as if by magic with fresh drinks for them all.

"So, Ben," Lucien said, "what do you do when you're not traveling the world?"

"That's most of the time," Ben admitted on a laugh. "The world traveling has only been the last few months. Before that, I hadn't gone farther from Australia than Bali. But to answer your question, I'm a nurse."

"Oh." Lucien sounded surprised. "In a hospital?"

Ben shook his head. "No. Well, not anymore. I do private nursing. Basically, I look after people in their own homes."

Lucien tipped his head forward and studied Ben over his sunglasses. "That must be interesting. Do you live in the house with them?"

"Sometimes. I did for my last job, but some of the other ones, especially when the patient has family living with them, I don't need to." Ben thought fondly of Mrs. K. and her horror when her grandson had suggested moving in to "help out." It had only been the insistence that she paid Ben to look after her already and wouldn't want to deprive him of his income—which had made Ben struggle to hide his laughter—that had convinced the young man his assistance wasn't needed.

"Are you backpacking, then?" Malik asked, his brow furrowed. "Where are you staying?" Unsaid but implied was that there weren't any backpacker hostels in Monaco —not the supercheap kind, anyway.

"At the Fairmont." At their clear surprise, Ben grinned. "I'm not backpacking."

"Clearly not." Lucien's curiosity was obvious in his voice. "Well, I'm going to hope we've already achieved friendship and ask an unspeakably rude question, then."

Ben laughed outright. He really liked these guys. "You're wondering how I can afford this trip, right? Because three months in Europe staying at hotels like the Fairmont doesn't come cheap, and nurses don't get paid that much."

Lucien nodded. "And you can't be old enough to have that much money in life savings," he added.

"Well, I'm also going to hope we've already achieved friendship and that you don't get offended when I say I got money the same way you all did—by inheriting it."

The three men laughed, Malik more loudly than the others. "That doesn't offend us at all," he assured Ben. "You're a trust fund baby too?" His eyes skimmed over Ben's outfit in a way that Ben thought could have been insulting if Malik had been someone else, especially considering how much Ben had paid for these clothes.

Although, considering Léo's car and apartment, Malik's yacht, and the fact that Ben didn't even recognize the brand decal on Lucien's sunglasses, he figured they probably paid a lot more for their clothes.

The very thought made him feel vaguely ill.

"I'm not a trust fund baby," he answered. "My last client was a wealthy widow. She left me some money in her will. She loved to travel, and we talked a lot about all the places she'd been, so I decided to spend some of it on a trip."

Lucien raised an eyebrow. "It must have been a good sum. And you must be an excellent nurse. Her family didn't object?"

Ben shook his head. "She was really quite wealthy, and what she left me was just a tiny piece of her estate. She left her family some cash too, but mostly they got the really good shares and investments and stuff. What they make in interest off those every year is about five times what she left me."

"I have to admit to being curious," Malik said, smiling that smile that made Ben want to just agree with anything he said. "May I be incredibly crass and ask how much she left you?"

Ben took another gulp from his martini. "Sure, why not? Friends tell each other this stuff, right? Fifty million."

Lucien spat out his drink, and Léo sat up abruptly.

"How much?" Malik asked incredulously.

Ben blinked. "Oh come on," he protested. "I've done my research online. Or Dani has. I know how much Léo's apartment and this yacht and the champagne cost. That kind of money is nothing to you guys."

One of the magic stewards appeared to give Lucien a hand towel and replace his drink, and Malik took advantage of the opportunity to knock back the rest of his and give the man the empty glass. Another one was supplied, and Ben looked around, wondering where it had come from.

"It's not nothing, exactly," Léo said slowly. "But yes, we have... more than that. It's just... it seems...."

"It's an incredibly generous bequest," Ben supplied, rescuing him. Unlike Malik and Lucien, Léo didn't seem willing to take advantage of the friendship clause and discuss the "crass"—who used that word, anyway?—topic of money. "But like I said, Mrs. K. was really quite wealthy, and I was her constant companion for three years. I monitored her health, helped her wash, dress, eat, I read to her, rubbed lotion on her skin, made sure she had her medications, and about a million other things. You form a pretty close bond after all that, and she and I had just clicked from the moment we met anyway." He shrugged. "She never mentioned that she'd added me to her will. I was pretty surprised when her solicitor told me I was a beneficiary, and downright shocked when he told me what I'd inherited. I was going to refuse it, at first, because it felt a little weird. But her kids insisted. She went through three nurses before me, because she could be a bit particular about things, and they were worried she'd have to go into a nursing home, which she would have hated. So they said I'd earned it, and then Dani told me to shut up and take it, so I did."

"And decided to spend a chunk in tribute to her by visiting the places she loved," Léo said, smiling. Ben nodded and leaned over to grab some cheese from the platter on the small table beside him.

"Yep."

"What are you doing with the rest of it?" Lucien also helped himself to cheese, then washed it down with his martini.

"Dunno."

All three men froze. Ben studied the ridiculous tableau. Malik's drink was halfway to his mouth, and Lucien was leaning toward the cheese again. Léo unfroze first and pulled off his sunglasses.

"What do you mean, you don't know? Where's the money now?"

Ben gestured vaguely in what he imagined might be the direction of Australia. "In my bank account."

Malik set his glass down with a sharp *clink*. "Do you mean you put fifty million Australian dollars—that's what" —he glanced at Léo—"about thirty-five million euro?"

Léo nodded.

"Right, so you put all that money in a standard bank account and just *left* it?"

Ben shook his head. "I gave about fifteen million away. Some to family and close friends, some to charity."

"It's still a lot of money to just leave," Lucien said, almost gently. "Have you spoken to a financial advisor?"

Ben laughed. "I wouldn't even know how to find a financial advisor," he said, and tipped the remainder of his drink down his throat, feeling pleasantly mellow. He silently counted down the time before a steward appeared with another drink for him.

Four seconds. Impressive.

"You're in luck, then," Malik said. "Léo's one of the best money people in the world. I'm sure he'd be happy to give you some tips."

Ben blinked, confused, and turned to Léo. "You're a money person? What's a money person?"

"I manage investments and advise on matters related to finance," Léo said, that indulgent grin back on his face.

"Like, officially? But that wasn't on Wikipedia. They said you just bum around."

Lucien snorted. "You've been on Léo's Wikipedia page? It makes for interesting reading, doesn't it? I'm especially proud of some of the photos."

"*You* created the page?" Ben asked, gobsmacked. "I haven't seen it myself. Dani told me about it."

"I didn't create it, but I like to check in on it sometimes, make some updates. Malik's too."

"I don't know what's on Malik's yet," Ben confessed. "Dani looked at it, but we didn't get a chance to talk about it."

"Just let me know if you have any questions," Malik said wickedly. "In the meantime, we've veered off topic. Léo doesn't consult for just anyone, Ben. He manages the investment portfolios of select family and friends, and a few charities. It's not really public knowledge, so whoever's contributing to the Wikipedia page probably doesn't know."

"Oh," Ben said, then, "*Oh*. You do charity work. That's great!" Léo didn't just bum around. Sure, he didn't work full-time, but he *worked*. He had responsibilities beyond hosting parties, or whatever.

"Well, not really," Léo began, but Lucien hushed him.

"Of course you do. They are charities, and you advise on their finances without charging a fee. That's charity work." He turned to look at Ben. "Why is it so great?"

Ben took a celebratory gulp from his glass. His already awesome day had just become awesomer. Awe-som-er. Was that a word?

"Ben?"

He looked up to find them all staring. "Yeah?" he asked happily.

"Why are you saying 'awesomer' over and over?" Malik asked.

Ben felt his cheeks getting hot and wondered why. They were all friends, right? And what was a made-up word among friends?

He decided to ask.

"Made-up words can be used when we're all friends, right?"

Léo's lips twitched, and Malik laughed outright.

"Absolutely," Lucien assured him gravely.

Ben grinned. "Great!"

"Yes, it is great," Malik said. "Do you know what else is great? That Léo does charity work."

"Yes!" Ben exclaimed, reminded again that Léo wasn't just a playboy dilettante. People trusted him with their money. Probably huge amounts of money.

"And why is that so great, Ben?" Malik prompted.

"Because he's not just a bum living off family money," Ben explained. "He has...." He frowned, trying to remember exactly what he was trying to say. "Work ethic! He has a work ethic. And responsibilities."

"Is that important to you, Ben? Because Léo doesn't exactly work a sixty-hour week," Lucien commented.

Ben shook his head. "That's okay. He doesn't need to work to support himself, so why should he run himself into an early grave working sixty hours a week? But he has focus and responsibilities. Re-spon-si-bil-i-ties," he repeated, suddenly loving the sound of the word.

Léo chucked. "If you're quite done discussing me as though I weren't here, I think Ben and I are ready for a nap," he said.

Ben was instantly distracted. "A nap?" he asked, smiling seductively.

Lucien coughed and Malik stood abruptly and turned away.

"What... kind... of nap?"

Léo looked away for a second, then back. "The sleeping kind."

Ben pouted, and Léo leaned over and dropped a kiss on his mouth. "Later," he murmured, cheering Ben immensely.

He was cruising the Mediterranean on a private yacht

with three new friends, one of whom he had "later" plans with. It didn't get much better than that.

IT WAS late afternoon before they returned to the marina, sun-kissed and relaxed. Sailing with Léo and his friends had been an experience.

As the four of them strolled toward the valet stand, Ben realized something. "Hey, we've been drinking almost all day, but none of us are drunk," he announced. His nap, and the great food that had been waiting when he woke up, had fixed that.

"Well, you might be a little tipsy," Lucien said with a smile.

Ben thought about it for a second, then nodded. "I think you might be right about that," he agreed, twisting to look at Lucien and tripping. Léo caught him with a laugh and wrapped an arm around his waist. Ben melted against him and let the warmth flow through his body.

"Anyway," he said, dragging his brain back toward a semblance of rational thought, "except for me, nobody's had too much to drink. And the other night, Léo didn't get drunk, even though I did." He paused. "I've spent too much time drinking since I got to Monaco."

Malik and Lucien laughed and motioned to the valets while Léo dropped a kiss on the top of Ben's head. "The secret," Lucien explained, "is to always be drinking but never be drunk."

Ben nodded sagely. "That makes sense. How does one do that?"

Léo propped him against a wall and leaned down to kiss him properly. He tasted like martinis and canapés and sunshine, and Ben lost himself in the kiss, reaching up to run his hands through Léo's beautiful, silky dark hair.

Eventually, Léo pulled back, then leaned in again to drop one more kiss on Ben's lips. "One does that," he murmured, "by drinking slowly and not mixing drinks."

"And drinking often," Malik added from where he and Lucien were standing a few feet away. "You build up a tolerance."

Ben bit his lip. Léo made a growling sound, and Ben swung a startled gaze in his direction. The hungry look on his gorgeous face was all Ben's dick needed to sit up and beg.

"Er…." He trailed off, having completely lost his train of thought. *Alcohol.* Right. "So the trick is to be constantly sipping at a single type of alcohol?"

"Something like that," Lucien agreed as one of the valets pulled up in a sporty-looking car that Ben didn't recognize but that was probably ridiculously expensive. "Now, if you'll excuse me, I have a date tonight."

"Oh, I didn't know you were seeing someone," Ben said brightly. That was nice, that Lucien had someone, but it must be tricky since he lived in Paris.

"I'm not," Lucien announced cheerfully.

Ben was taken aback. "Then who's your date with?" he asked.

Lucien shrugged. "I don't know. I haven't met him yet." He waved airily over his shoulder as he got into his car.

Him? Huh. Lucien's gay. Ben's muddled brain found that both completely obvious and mildly surprising.

"Come on, Bunny," Léo said as another valet pulled up in his car. "Time to get home." He opened the passenger door while Ben latched on to what he'd said.

"Did you just call me Bunny?" He climbed into the car.

"I think Lucien called me that today too." He frowned, looking up at Léo. "Am I a bunny? I always imagined myself to be more of a…. Actually, I don't think I've ever considered myself to be any kind of animal." He leaned back in his seat, ignoring Malik's laughter as he pondered the situation, and Léo closed the car door. Moments later, the driver door opened and Léo slid into the car. Ben grinned at him as he started the car, and even though he was pretty sure he looked kind of foolish, Léo still reached over and took his hand as they pulled out onto the road.

"Am I a bunny?" Ben asked.

Léo hesitated. "Only in the best possible way," he finally said. Ben struggled to make sense of that and then gave up. Léo seemed to be saying it affectionately, and Ben was totally okay with pet names.

It didn't take long to get back to Léo's apartment building, and once they'd parked in Léo's reserved spot, they just sat for a moment.

"So, are you enjoying Monaco?" Léo asked, breaking the silence.

Ben smiled. "Yes," he said honestly. "Much more than I thought I would. I figured I'd spend a couple of days being lazy by the pool, see the aquarium, the casino, the Prince's Palace, and then be ready to move on. But this has been a real experience. I never would have thought of trying half the stuff I've done." He rolled his head against the seat to look at Léo. "That's because of you. I wouldn't have had nearly as much fun if I hadn't met you."

Léo smiled back at him, and something in Ben melted. It wasn't just the bronzed complexion, dark eyes, and sharp cheekbones that attracted him. It was that *smile*, the look in those eyes, as if Ben were amazing, as if he'd said something incredibly clever and Léo was lucky to be there with him.

He felt special.

"Are you going to stay a while longer?"

Ben looked away. "I haven't decided. Maybe." His heartbeat sped up. *Please let him want me to stay.*

"You should stay." Ben's gaze flicked back and met Léo's. "Spend some time with me."

Ben's stomach flipped with joyful anticipation.

"Okay."

Chapter Eight

"I can't believe you haven't taken him to dinner at Le Louis XV," Lucien chided Léo. "It's one of your favorite restaurants."

They were finishing brunch at the club, exactly two weeks after the first time they'd done so. This time, Léo had actually invited Malik and Lucien to join them— although admittedly at Ben's suggestion. Lucien was only in Monaco for two days, and Ben felt bad that he was monopolizing Léo's time and preventing him from hanging out with his friend.

"We haven't had the opportunity," Léo was saying. "And Ben has been cooking for me sometimes. It's nice to have home-cooked meals that I don't have to prepare. I'd forgotten how much I liked it."

"You should have a service come and cook for you," Malik suggested.

Ben tried not to react to the idea of paying someone to cook for you in your own home *all the time*. He knew Léo could cook, and quite well, since they'd prepared quite a few meals together. It seemed Malik couldn't—or didn't.

"I don't need a service," Léo said patiently.

"*Anyway*," Lucien interjected pointedly. "Since you've been unspeakably lazy on this matter, why don't we all go tonight? Ben will like the decor, I think, and definitely the food."

Léo shrugged. "I would never refuse Le Louis XV," he said, sitting back and letting the waiter clear his plate. "Ben, would you like to go?"

Ben smiled his thanks to the waiter and then turned to Léo and said, "To be honest, I have no idea what you're talking about."

Léo smiled, Malik laughed, and Lucien groaned.

"It's a restaurant," Léo told him, "at the Hotel de Paris."

"Which means it's probably an excellent restaurant, right?" When Ben had been planning his visit to Monaco, he'd looked into staying at the Hotel de Paris, which was where Mrs. K. had always stayed. He hadn't been able to bring himself to pay those rates for a hotel, no matter how good. The Fairmont wasn't cheap, but the difference worked out to about a hundred euro a night.

"It is indeed," Lucien assured him. "It also has three Michelin stars."

He was still trying to get his head around the idea that three Michelin stars was not what made these men consider a restaurant "excellent," when Léo said, "I think you'll enjoy it. Their wine cellar is wonderful."

Ben flushed. Although he hadn't been drunk since that day on the yacht, and was in fact mastering the art of drinking without becoming intoxicated (how Dani had laughed when he'd told her about that!), he was still worried that Léo might think him a lush. But the wine he'd been drinking here was *so good*, and even though he knew —after battling Léo several times for the right to pay when they went out—that it was so good because it cost so much, he hadn't been able to switch back to something more… economical.

"Okay, we should go," he agreed. He'd never eaten at a Michelin-starred restaurant before, not even one with only one star, and he figured it would make for another great story to tell when he got home.

Whenever that would be. Right now, he didn't even have plans to leave Monaco for Italy, much less leave Europe to go back to Australia.

"We'll go tonight, then," Malik declared. "I have a date for drinks at five, so shall we say eight?"

"Doesn't it depend on what time we can get a reservation?" Ben asked, and then felt stupid as realization hit. One couldn't just decide to eat at a Michelin-starred restaurant that same day. He'd bet the place booked up weeks, if not months, in advance. But his dining companions had gone silent. Léo and Malik were conspicuously focused on the table, and Lucien was looking at him curiously.

They weren't even thinking about reservations, or the fact that the restaurant might be fully booked.

Ben sighed. "You were planning to just turn up and commandeer a table, weren't you?" he asked resignedly.

Lucien raised a brow. "Commandeer? You make it sound as though we were going to evict people who were already eating," he protested. "We will go to the restaurant, and they will give us a table if one is available."

Léo choked slightly—on what, Ben didn't know. The two of them had had this discussion several times over the past two weeks and had now settled into an uneasy truce on the subject.

"Lucien," Ben began patiently, "have you ever gone to

a restaurant and been turned away because a table wasn't available?"

Lucien paused and appeared to think. "Well—no, but there have been times I've had to wait."

"How long?" Ben pressed, pretty sure that the restaurants Lucien went to didn't have benches by the door for people to wait on for an hour.

Sure enough, Lucien shrugged. "A few minutes? Once it was as long as five. I remember because my date was most unimpressed by the service." Malik visibly winced. Ben guessed Léo had discussed Ben's opinion on this with him.

"Right, so occasionally you've had to wait as little as five minutes for a table in a top-class restaurant. Now, these restaurants, Lucien—are there ever lots of empty tables in them?"

From the expression on Lucien's face, he was becoming aware of Ben's point.

"No," he sighed. "All right, I understand. You think other people are being turned away in our favor, even if they had reservations."

"Yes."

"And this is something you don't approve of?"

Ben sucked in a deep breath. *He's a product of his upbringing,* he reminded himself. *You like Lucien. He's a good guy— when he's not being all Marie Antoinette.*

Under the table, Léo reached out and took his hand. "Why don't I call the restaurant and see if an arrangement can be made?" he suggested diplomatically, squeezing Ben's hand. "I will make certain nobody is inconvenienced on our behalf."

"I'll do it," Malik said, pulling out his phone and standing. Use of phones was strictly forbidden in the restaurant at the club.

Ben smiled at them both. "Thank you," he said.

Malik winked at him and walked away.

"I'm sorry if I have offended you," Lucien offered. "I never thought that maybe the tables were meant for someone else. I have just always...." He shrugged, and Ben chuckled.

"Relax, Lucien, I'm not offended. It's just something for you to consider in future. Maybe make sure nobody's actual meal is being interrupted."

Lucien laughed. "I had not considered that, but how awful if while my date was complaining about the wait to be seated, the waiters were chasing people away from their food and resetting the table."

Ben winced, and Léo said, "If it helps, I'm sure the people being chased away were suitably compensated by the restaurant."

Thinking about it, he had to agree. "Otherwise there probably would be some really rotten reviews online."

Malik strolled back toward them. "Eight o'clock," he confirmed. "They were fully booked, Ben, but I had them check the reservation book, and one of the parties was an associate of Léo's father. I phoned him and promised him a case of excellent brandy and my cooking service to have a romantic evening in instead, along with Léo's undying gratitude." The last was said with a mocking smirk at Léo, who sighed.

"Is that going to be a problem?" Ben asked worriedly, and Léo smiled at him and leaned over for a kiss.

"No. It just means the next time I am cornered at a party, I must ensure I am polite," he assured him, then looked at Malik. "Who?"

"Max Valverde."

"That's not so bad," Léo told Ben, who was pretty sure

Léo was incapable of being rude at a party anyway. "All right, then. Dinner at eight."

EARLY IN THE AFTERNOON, Léo ensconced himself in the room he used as an office, and Ben flopped down on the couch to call Dani. She'd had a lunch date that day, and he was eager to hear all the details.

"Don't bother getting excited, it was a complete waste of time" was how she answered the phone, and Ben made a face.

"Nooo! You were so looking forward to it. I thought you said he was great?"

"Apparently he's only great in five-minute increments. This is the last time I go on a date with someone I meet at my daily coffee stop. I've never been so bored in my life."

Ben sighed. "Oh well. At least that's one more frog off the list. Your prince has gotta turn up soon, right?"

Dani laughed, and when she spoke again she sounded a lot lighter. "Yeah, I'll find him eventually. So, what's up with you? You were having brunch this morning, right?"

"Yep, with Malik and Lucien. It was good. They're a lot of fun. I think you'd really like them. And we're going out for dinner tonight."

"Anywhere special?" Dani's interest was definitely caught. One of her favorite pastimes lately seemed to be looking up the places Léo took Ben and then telling Ben all about them, including which famous people were known to frequent them.

"A restaurant at the Hotel de Paris, Louis something. It's one of Léo's favorites, apparently, and supposed to be a big deal." There was a moment's silence, presumably while Dani did a Google search—since he couldn't hear the clack of a keyboard, he guessed she was using her tablet—then a low whistle.

"Three Michelin stars? Wow. And you should see the pictures of this place. Super fancy."

"I'm not looking," he told her. "I want to experience it for the first time tonight."

"Mmm," she said absently. "What are you going to wear?"

He shrugged, even though he knew she couldn't see him. "Not sure yet. Pants and one of those shirts you made me buy?" He was aware of the edge of resentment in his voice. Once his stay in Monaco had extended, Dani had insisted he go shopping again for more clothes. He was loath to admit that she'd been right, that he'd needed everything she'd made him buy, what with his new social life—and he probably needed more.

"Ben, this place is pretty fancy. They don't set an exact dress code on the website, but it says, and I quote, 'Jacket recommended during the winter and appreciated during the summer.' Maybe check with Léo and see what he's wearing."

Ben huffed and let his head fall back against the couch. "I hate clothes," he muttered.

Dani made a sympathetic noise. "But you like the boat shoes, right?"

"I did *not* say that," he said, getting up to ask Léo what he should wear, as though he were five years old and needed his mum's help choosing an outfit. "I said they were surprisingly comfortable."

"And that you haven't bothered to buy another pair of runners," Dani reminded him.

He rolled his eyes. "Nobody wears runners here unless they're playing tennis or something," he complained. "Can you picture me on a tennis court?"

She laughed. "Picturing it now!"

Ben ignored her, lowering the hand holding the phone as he knocked lightly on Léo's open office door with the other. His handsome lover looked up and smiled, and there was a corresponding melty feeling in Ben's stomach.

"Hey," he said. "Sorry to interrupt, but Dani and I were just wondering what the dress code is for dinner tonight."

"Hello, Dani," Léo said, and Ben lifted the phone back to his ear.

"Did you hear that?"

"Yes," Dani said. "Say hi back."

"She says hello," Ben relayed, feeling slightly ridiculous. "Dress code?"

Léo shrugged. "I will wear a suit," he replied. "I imagine Malik and Lucien will also."

Ben's heart sank. "A suit," he repeated. "But on the website they say a jacket is optional."

Léo paused, and Ben got the feeling he was choosing his next words carefully. "They will not turn you away if you do not have a jacket in the summer," he said finally. "But they... do not look kindly on it."

Against his ear, Dani said, "In other words, they'll look down on you and maybe treat you like shit. Benji, we're going suit shopping."

"I wish you'd stop calling me that," he said weakly, hating the very thought of buying a suit, and then when Léo raised an eyebrow, he added, "Dani."

"Ask Léo where's the best place to get a suit at short notice," she urged, and thinking of how he didn't even recognize the labels on some of Léo's clothes, Ben shut that down quickly.

"Thanks, Léo. Dani and I are going to go shopping, I'll be back soon."

Léo's smirk told Ben he wasn't fooling anyone. "Do you want me to come?"

"Yes!" Dani exclaimed.

Ben backed into the corridor. "Uh, no, that's cool."

Léo chuckled and hit a few keys on his computer before getting up. "Come on, Ben. I know just where we should go."

Dani cheered, and Ben knew Léo had heard because his smile widened. "You'll need your shoes," he said.

Ben looked down at his feet. "I'm wearing shoes," he pointed out. The boat shoes, in fact, which he was getting way too attached to.

"No," Léo said. "You need the shoes you will wear with the suit. They will need to make sure your trousers are the correct length."

"Yeah, Ben. I can't believe you didn't know that," Dani jeered.

Ben kept his mouth shut and went to get his dress shoes from Léo's bedroom. He briefly considered changing into them, but they'd look dumb with what he was wearing, so he just carried them instead.

He let himself be led out of the apartment and to the car, Dani chattering in his ear the whole time, warning him not to let anyone dress him in brown, because it was *not* his color.

A brown suit? Do people even wear those anymore? He paused to consider it carefully and realized that he had actually seen a few men wearing brown suits, but the brown wasn't… brown. It was like milk chocolate, or espresso, or—

"You're quiet," Léo commented, and Ben realized he was parking the car. Wow, he'd really tuned out. Although, Dani was still burbling away about something, so maybe that wasn't the worst thing.

"Uh, just distracted," he said, trying not to sound like he was on his way to his own execution.

"Distracted by what?" Dani asked.

"Do I really need you here if I've got Léo with me?" Ben asked.

Léo chuckled, and Dani squawked.

"Don't you even *think* of hanging up on me, Benji!" she scolded. "I will call you back and keep calling until the very sound of a ringing phone makes you break out in a sweat."

"Don't call me Benji," he said. "And I already break out in a sweat when I see your name on the display." He saw Léo mouthing *Benji* and closed his eyes for a moment. *Please let this not become a thing.*

"Come," Léo said, and got out of the car. Ben followed suit and trailed Léo out of the parking garage. Street parking in Monaco was rarely possible, he'd learned, but resident parking was more readily available than it was for tourists.

Soon they stood on the footpath in front of an unassuming shopfront. Well, unassuming for Monaco. There were two male mannequins in the window, both dressed in suits that even to Ben looked expensive. Until he'd come to Europe and begun staying in classy hotels, he'd always thought a suit was a suit, but once he'd seen the suits rich people wore, the way they fit and the sheen of the fabric, he'd realized there was in fact a difference. He just wasn't sure it was a difference he cared about.

He hadn't seen Léo in an actual suit yet, but his pants and jackets were the nicest Ben had ever seen.

He gulped, then realized that Léo was watching him and Dani had gone quiet.

"Benji?" Léo asked, and Ben scowled.

"She only calls me that to be annoying. My name isn't even Benjamin."

Dani huffed a laugh in his ear.

"What is your name, then?" Léo looked genuinely curious, and Ben took hope that the whole "Benji" thing wasn't going to catch on.

"Benedict. Benedict Andrew Adams."

"Benedict," Léo repeated, and the sound of his name on Léo's lips did things to Ben that he wasn't sure were appropriate for a public street. "Well, Benedict, let us get you a suit."

As they moved toward the shop door, Dani said, "You know, I never realized, but your initials spell *baa*." She made a sheep sound, and Ben swore to himself that in his next life, his best friend was going to be a sweet, docile sort who baked cookies and listened to his troubles without offering cheeky commentary.

Sure. That's going to happen.

They stopped at the glass door, and Léo pressed a buzzer set discreetly on the wall. The young man sitting at what looked like an antique writing desk looked up and immediately stood, smiling. He hurried over and unlocked the door, flung it open, and gestured them inside.

"Monsieur Artois," he greeted warmly, and then rattled something off in French that sounded welcoming and enthusiastic, but made no sense to Ben.

Maybe I should learn French.

Am I going to be here long enough for it to matter? After all, French isn't going to be much use to me in Italy, is it?

That thought was vaguely depressing for some reason, so he pushed it aside and refocused in time to hear Léo say, "In English, please, Martin. Ben does not speak French."

The man turned to Ben. "My apologies, monsieur. I am Martin, and it is a pleasure to meet you."

"Ben Adams," Ben muttered, thrown a little off by the way Martin scanned him from top to bottom, as though he were mentally sizing Ben for a suit. And speaking of suits... where were they? The store was fitted out like an elegant living room, with the aforementioned desk, a pair of sofas facing each other with a coffee table in between, a few armchairs scattered around, a drinks cart, and an assortment of sideboards and end tables. Toward the rear was a set of ornate double doors. The only indication that clothes were sold here were the mannequins in the window.

He had a feeling this suit was going to be an "investment."

"What may I assist you with today, gentlemen?" Martin asked.

"We are dining at Le Louis XV this evening," Léo said, "and Ben requires a suit."

"Of course." Martin smiled. "Do you have any preference for color or style, monsieur?"

"Er... not brown?" Ben said. In his ear, Dani laughed, and he realized that Martin had not reacted in any way to the fact that Ben was holding his mobile to his ear. "Excuse me," he said, and turned away to hiss at Dani, "I'm hanging up now. Léo will make sure I buy the right thing, but honestly, Dani, if you could see this place, you wouldn't worry. I don't think they sell the 'wrong' thing here."

"Fine," Dani said. "I'll leave you in Léo's and Martin's hands, but I want pictures later."

"Sure, whatever," Ben promised, aware that she'd hold him to that but willing to do anything to make this experience at least a tiny bit less like a sitcom. He bid Dani a hasty goodbye and disconnected to the sound of her laughter. "Sorry about that," he said, turning back to Léo and Martin. Léo was smiling openly, but Martin's amusement was visible only in the twinkle in his eye.

"I will fetch Monsieur Carrere," he announced, and hurried over to and through the double doors.

"Why is he fetching Monsieur Carrere?" Ben asked Léo, and then felt like an idiot for actually using the word "fetch." Although, come to think of it, it was a perfectly good word, and had a pretty good sound to it. Fetch. *Fetch*. Feeeeeeetch.

"Because Monsieur Carrere is the couturier," Léo answered.

Ben tipped his head. "Couturier?" He was pretty sure that had something to do with clothes—couture fashion, right?—but he didn't think he'd ever heard the word actually used before.

"The owner of the establishment, designer, and Master Tailor. He has done design work for Caraceni and Anderson & Sheppard, but prefers to keep his customer base small and work with them personally."

Ben swallowed hard. He didn't recognize those designers, which meant either they were completely unknown—not likely, given the way Léo had rattled off the names—or they were way out of his comfort zone.

He forced a smile and nodded, and Léo laughed. "It will be fine. You'll see."

The double doors opened and Martin came back out, accompanied by a graying middle-aged man who could only be described as distinguished. His hair was faultlessly tidy, his wire-rimmed glasses effortlessly classy, and his suit was… well, it was clearly designed and made just for him.

"Monsieur Artois, so nice to see you again," he said in barely accented English, which meant Martin had obviously given him a rundown. "And Monsieur Adams, a pleasure to meet you."

"And you," Ben said bravely, keeping his smile pasted on his face.

Léo stepped forward and shook the tailor/designer/*couturier's* hand. "Monsieur Carrere, it is always a pleasure," he said smoothly. "We are in dire need of your assistance. Tonight we dine at Le Louis XV, and Ben does not have a suit with him."

Monsieur Carrere ran a professional gaze over Ben, and he couldn't help wondering if the man could guess that the single suit he had at home, bought for Mrs. K.'s funeral, was probably not up to the standards of the men in the room.

"It is not ideal," Monsieur Carrere said. "A suit should be designed and tailored for the wearer, but there is no time for that. I have some I use for display that may be acceptable, and we will of course tailor them for you now, but...." He sniffed, as if having to custom tailor an existing suit was on par with having to serve leftover scrambled eggs at a dinner for royalty.

"Anything you can provide, even in such inopportune circumstances, would be better than an off-the-rack option elsewhere," Léo said, and Monsieur Carrere shuddered.

"The charcoal pinstripe, I think," he said to Martin, who disappeared back through the doors. "Monsieur Adams, if you will come this way." He swept an arm toward the doors, and Ben shot a terrified look at Léo, who grinned.

"Shall we?" he said, and took Ben's arm, leading him through what Ben later privately dubbed the gates of hell.

The back area was not so different from the front. Again there was comfortable-looking yet elegant seating, and a drinks cart. Back here, though, were several mannequins dressed in suits and two clothing racks containing suit bags—which presumably held suits. There were also three large full-length mirrors, ornately framed. A discreet door was off to the side, and Ben bet that was where the real work happened. Martin came through the door a moment later, carrying a suit on a hanger.

"Monsieur Adams, if you will remove your clothing?"

Ben flushed but obediently stripped out of the pants he'd worn to the club that morning. He wasn't sure what they had against jeans there, but the restaurant had an "unspoken" dress code. He kept his shirt on, and Monsieur Carrere make a tsking sound and disappeared through the door to the back.

He took the pants Martin handed him and immediately wished he'd washed his hands first. The material was… he couldn't even think of a word, except it was soft and silky and smooth and he wanted to roll around in it. Instead, he slipped them on and fastened them.

"And the shoes, monsieur?" Martin requested. Ben silently put on his dress shoes. He was just tying the laces when Monsieur Carrere came back carrying a shirt in a pewter color.

"Try this, monsieur," he ordered.

Ben took it meekly and looked at Léo for help against these bossy men. His lover had obviously helped himself to the drinks cart, and was settled in an armchair, drink in hand, looking for all the world as though he were watching a play. He smiled at Ben, and Ben knew there would be no aid from that quarter. He sighed and stripped off his shirt, replacing it with the one supplied— which admittedly felt heavenly. It needed cuff links, though, and the sleeves flapped about his wrists as he buttoned it.

No sooner had Ben opened his mouth than Martin handed him a pair of plain gold cuff links.

"We keep these for fittings," Martin said.

Ben looked at Léo again. "That won't help me tonight," he said.

Léo shrugged. "I can lend you a pair. Or we can purchase some on the way home."

"I know just the pair for this suit," Monsieur Carrere said, reaching in to fasten the very top button of the shirt and forcing Ben to lift his chin. "At Ciribelli. I will phone and have them sent over."

"Thank you, monsieur," Léo replied.

"Thank you," Ben echoed, not sure if he was actually thankful. Dani had mentioned Ciribelli last week, among the tons of other trivia she'd dug up about Monaco. Still, good jewelry was an investment, right?

Monsieur Carrere slipped away again, and Martin gave him the jacket. Ben slipped it on. To be honest, if he'd been shopping on his own, he would have said the suit fit perfectly, which was pretty freaky since nobody had asked his size or measured him, and he'd have called it done and bought the thing. But Martin was kneeling before him, having produced pins from somewhere, and was fussing with the hems and inseams of his pants. Ben took the opportunity to examine the suit more closely. He could also see himself in one of the mirrors. He had to admit, it looked good. It was a kind of charcoal-on-charcoal pinstripe, single breasted, with lapels that were neither too wide nor too narrow.

Martin stood and began pinning the jacket, directing Ben to lift his arms, lower them, turn this way and that, relax his shoulders, and do the hokeypokey. Well, not really, but it felt like it. Monsieur Carrere came back again and joined Martin, fussing until Ben was ready to smack them both. Eventually, they stepped back.

"All right," Monsieur said. "We will need several hours to make the alterations." A buzzer went in the front room. "Ah, that will be the cuff links. Martin?" As Martin headed toward the front of the store, Monsieur helped Ben slide out of the jacket. "I have a cravat that was designed for this suit. I will fetch it." There was that word again—fetch. And really, a cravat? He was actually supposed to wear a cravat? Monsieur took the jacket and went through the door to the back room, and Léo stood, putting his drink down on a side table.

"Even with pins stuck in everywhere, that suit makes you look edible," he said in a low voice, strolling toward Ben with a gleam in his eye that made Ben shiver. He stopped a hairsbreadth away and leaned down, feathering his lips against Ben's so lightly that Ben almost couldn't stand it. He sucked in a breath and rose onto his tiptoes, pressing his mouth to Léo's in a proper kiss. Desire surged as it always did, and within moments he was wrapped tightly in Léo's arms, trying his best not to grind despite desperately wanting to.

He tore his mouth away. "Léo, not here. They'll come back," he panted. Léo dropped his head to rest his forehead against Ben's, drawing in a deep breath. Then he let go, turned, and walked back to his chair, dropping into it just as Martin came back. His gaze took them both in, and a tiny smile quirked his lips, but he said nothing, instead crossing to Ben and helping him insert the delivered cuff links—which even Ben had to admire. Once they were secure, he pulled out the pins again and began his little routine, and Ben lifted his gaze to the mirror.

And winced. His hair was mussed, his face flushed, his eyes overbright. He definitely did not look like he had been waiting innocently for Martin's return.

Monsieur bustled in, cravat in hand. It turned out to look pretty much like a regular tie, not the poufy scarf thing his cousin had worn to get married. The color was ivory, with a subtle sheen, which surprised him but actually looked great against the shirt.

Finally, *finally*, the fussing was done and Ben was back in his own clothes. Léo assured Monsieur Carrere that they would be back in three hours, and then led Ben out onto the street.

"Coffee?" he asked.

"Um, sure," Ben said. "Don't I need to pay?" They strolled back toward the car.

Léo shook his head. "Monsieur will send a bill."

Ben blinked. "So... I won't know how much it costs until I get the bill?"

Léo raised an eyebrow at him over the car. "If you need to know how much it costs, you cannot afford it," he said, and got into the driver seat, leaving Ben frowning.

"That is not helpful," he muttered, and pulled out his phone to text Dani.

> SOS—what can you tell me about designer/tailor Carrere?

He got in the car and did his seat belt up as Léo started the engine. His phone dinged.

> Checking now.

At least he could count on Dani.

"What about the cuff links?" he asked as Léo pulled out of the parking spot.

"Monsieur will add them to the bill and then ensure that Ciribelli is paid. He will also make sure you have the necessary papers for insurance."

As Ben digested the fact that he was about to buy cuff links that needed to be *insured*, his phone dinged again.

> Top designer and tailor of bespoke suits. Best of the best, doesn't take just any client. Must be referred or invited. Way to go, Benji!

Fuck.

> Any idea of cost?

> Didn't you just buy a suit from there?

> Yes, but Léo says I will be sent a bill, and I have no idea how much for!!! Can you also look at cuff links from Ciribelli?

> LOL! This could only happen to you! No prices attached to Carrere that I can see, but other bespoke designers like him seem to start at $4k, most around the $6k mark and up. Ciribelli has no prices on their website. Just go with the flow!

> Thanks, you're no help. And don't call me Benji.

> Love you! xx

He dropped his phone to his lap with a sigh.

"Dani didn't make you feel better?" Léo asked.

"Not really," Ben said, and then wanted to bite his tongue. "I'm sorry. I'm being a dick. The suit is... beautiful. I've never worn anything so nice. I just... I'm not used to not worrying about money. In my life, you don't buy something without knowing how much it costs and weighing whether it's worth it."

"Ah, but you're not in your life right now," Léo pointed out. "New experiences, remember? Also, I think you will find even when you get home that your life has changed. Fifty million small changes."

Ben paused to consider that. "I don't have fifty million anymore," he reminded Léo, who laughed.

"Even with what you've given away, you have a substantial amount left."

True.

Léo brought the car to a stop and put it in Park, and Ben looked around. They were at the valet parking area in the Place du Casino. He blinked.

"Where are we having coffee?"

Léo nodded toward the Café de Paris.

"Would you like some ice cream?"

Chapter Nine

B en and Léo entered the restaurant at fifteen minutes after eight and were greeted effusively. The maître d'hôtel chattered away in French, and when Léo glanced at Ben and opened his mouth to request that the man speak in English, as he had many times over the past couple of weeks, Ben shook his head. It didn't really matter right now; the man was likely just fawning over Léo and—yep, he was gesturing across the restaurant. Lucien and Malik were probably already seated.

They followed him on a path winding through the widely spaced tables, and Léo nodded to several people, stopping once to kiss an elderly lady's hand. They finally arrived at their table, which was by the window (Ben suspected it was the best one in the place) and sure enough, Malik and Lucien were waiting.

"Sorry we're late," Ben said as they were seated and a waiter appeared to fuss over napkin placement and fill their water glasses. "I couldn't find the key to my room, and the reception desk at the hotel was really busy. I think it was a tour group or something. Anyway, that put me way behind." He picked up his menu, opened it, and tried not to gasp. Millet was some kind of grain, right? So how could millet, mushrooms, and cabbage as a first course cost *ninety euros*? It wasn't even one of those super-expensive special species of mushroom, just "wood mushrooms."

Léo's hand closed over Ben's menu and pulled it away. Ben met his gaze, doing his best not to look shocked. "Many little changes and new experiences," Léo said gently. "Why don't I order for you?"

Ben took a deep breath. "That's a good idea," he answered. Léo was right. New experiences. How often was he going to eat at a three-Michelin-starred restaurant in Monaco in the company of three suave billionaires?

Although, he felt like he'd been asking himself "how often will I" an awful lot lately. And since he'd already been in Monaco a lot longer than he'd expected—with no departure date in sight yet—there was a pretty good chance he'd end up repeating some of these experiences. Like eating at the yacht club. He'd done that four times now.

And having sex with Léo. He'd lost track of how many times he'd done *that*. Including a quickie that afternoon between ice cream at Café de Paris and picking up his new suit.

He was distracted from his thoughts when Léo pressed his wineglass into his hand. Apparently, while he'd been pondering sex with Léo, the sommelier had come, gone to collect the wine, and served it. There were no menus on the table, so they'd probably ordered too, and there was a plate in front of him containing a bite-sized morsel of... something. He knew from eating out with Léo at other posh restaurants that it was an amuse-bouche, a single hors d'oeuvre offered with the compliments of the chef.

He ate it, not sure what it was, but it tasted good. Some kind of preserved meat and pickled vegetable?

"You're deep in thought," Lucien said, and Ben tried hard not to blush, because most of his thoughts had centered on sex. From the heat in his face and the twinkle in Lucien's eye, he'd failed, but they all pretended it wasn't happening—except for the sidelong glance Léo gave him. For some reason, Léo liked it when he got flustered.

"I was just thinking that I need to do some washing soon," he improvised. "I've been sending my things out with Léo's"—because Léo didn't have a washing machine, and there were literally no self-service coin laundromats in Monaco—"but at the hotel tonight, I realized there's some stuff there that could do with a wash."

"Washing," Malik said in a carefully neutral tone. "Sure. That's a nice suit, by the way."

"Thank you," Ben said. "I got it today." It really was a nice suit, and clearly Monsieur Carrere and Martin knew more about making suits than he did, because once they'd finished altering it, it had looked amazing on Ben. The changes weren't big, but they had a big impact.

"Carrere?" Lucien asked, and Léo nodded. "You can tell. Did you do anything else interesting today?"

"Just ice cream and coffee," Léo said, and the heat in Ben's cheeks flared again. In an effort to be nonchalant, he looked at the wineglass in his hand. The liquid inside was a pale golden color. Léo was always particular about matching wine to food, so he figured he'd be eating something that went with white wine. He took a sip, and as usual when Léo ordered the wine, it was wonderful. Light and dry without the bitterness he'd always associated with dry wine in the past.

"I like this," he said, and Léo smiled.

"It's Lucien's favorite wine," he said, and across the table Lucien lifted his glass in salute before taking a sip.

"So," Malik said, "you never said this morning, Lucien, if there's any interesting gossip from Paris."

Lucien made a face. "Nothing. Everybody is being boring. The most interesting thing I have to report is that I saw your sister-in-law, Léo, and she's starting to show."

Show? Show what? Oh! Ben blinked. "Your sister-in-law is pregnant?" he asked, then wondered if it was even her first pregnancy. Maybe Léo already had nephews or nieces—or both?

"Yes," Léo said. "I think the baby is due in October. My father is thrilled—the line of succession will be ensured." He spoke very dryly.

"Have you been ordered back to Paris for the birth?" Malik asked, and Léo shook his head.

"Not yet. I think he knows I don't need to be there."

Their first course arrived, and Ben studied his plate as it was set in front of him. Some sort of seafood thing with prawns. It looked good, and he'd yet to dislike anything Léo had ordered him, so he waited until everyone had been served and then picked up his fork. He was pretty sure it was the right one; he'd gotten quite a bit of experience selecting cutlery lately.

The food was good. In fact, it was so good that Ben tuned out the conversation and focused entirely on what he was putting in his mouth. By the time he'd swallowed the last morsel and looked up, he'd completely lost track of what they'd been talking about. Quickly determining that it wasn't something that interested him, he looked around the restaurant instead. Lucien had been right; he did like the decor. All cream and gold, with ornate plaster moldings and an absolutely gorgeous ceiling. He wanted to tip his head back and study it in more detail, but he was already getting the occasional sidelong glance from some of the other tables, and didn't want to look out of place.

Again.

"Ben?" Malik interrupted his hopefully surreptitious inspection of the ceiling.

"Yes?"

Their waiter came and began clearing the first course.

"You said something before that made me curious."

Ben thought back over what he'd said so far this evening. Nothing very interesting, that was for sure. "What was that?"

"You were talking about your hotel room."

Not sure where Malik was going with this, Ben said, "Yeees? Usually when you go to a place where you don't have a home, you stay in a hotel. You knew I was doing that, Malik."

Lucien snorted and Léo smiled. Malik grinned. "No, what I mean is, I didn't know you still had the room at the Fairmont. You've been at Léo's so often, I thought you'd given it up."

Oh my God, he thinks I'm a freeloader! Ben turned to Léo, stricken. "I-I can stay at the hotel more. I didn't mean to imp—"

"Hush," Léo said. "I don't want you to stay at the hotel more. I like having you with me." He glared at his cousin.

"I'm sorry, Ben, I'm not explaining myself well," Malik apologized. "I didn't mean that you shouldn't stay with Léo. In fact, quite the opposite."

As Ben's heartbeat returned to normal, he reached for his wine and tried to work out what Malik was saying. The opposite of not staying with Léo was... staying with Léo.

He shook his head. "What?"

Malik sighed. "Why don't you just stay with Léo?"

Ben blinked. "Well... because we've only known each other a few weeks. And... he hasn't.... He doesn't...." He could feel his face getting hot.

"Ben," Léo said, and Ben forced himself to meet his lover's warm gaze. "Why don't you give up that room and move in with me? It's been days since you even went back to the hotel, anyway, and I hated it when you did."

Ben's smile was so wide he thought his cheeks might crack. He probably looked like a fool, but he didn't care. Léo wanted him to stay with him!

"Sure, okay," he said, going for casual and pretty sure he failed miserably. "I'd like that."

Their main course arrived, and Ben dug in cheerfully. Good food, pleasant surroundings, great company, and positive developments in his relationship with Léo. What more could he ask?

Apparently, for them to be the only people in the restaurant.

They were halfway through their main course when the elderly lady Léo had greeted earlier approached their table.

"Léonard," she demanded imperiously when she was still six feet away, and Léo, Malik, and Lucien all rose immediately. Ben scrambled to do so also; no way was he going to be the only one sitting. He'd stand out like a shag on a rock.

"Madame," Léo said, inclining his head. He added something in French, and Ben felt the first inkling of dread. Léo had become very particular about people only speaking English when Ben was around, and the fact that he wasn't even attempting to insist on it now told Ben the woman must be a formidable force in his life.

He studied her while trying not to stare, which he

considered a huge accomplishment. She was not dressed in typical "old lady" clothes, but at the same time, he didn't get the feeling she was trying to look younger. Her evening gown was of an obviously expensive fabric, with just a hint of shimmer and sparkle, as was her shawl. The heels on her shoes were not terribly high, but Ben figured any kind of heel at her age was something to celebrate. Speaking of age... he tried to work out how old she was. Definitely over seventy, but based on her looks she could really be anywhere up to ninety. Her hair was swept into an impeccable updo set off with sparkly hair clips that he was pretty sure were real diamonds. In fact, all her jewelry—earrings, necklace, bracelets, rings—were probably real gems. The woman was walking around wearing a fortune. She wasn't alone, was she? He seemed to remember someone else had been eating with her.

Ben glanced around and saw a middle-aged man who looked vaguely familiar waiting by the door.

The woman was speaking to Lucien now, her tone curt and imperious, and Lucien was nodding, murmuring something that could have been a platitude. Malik looked almost green when she turned on him, although he did manage to pull out his charming smile. It actually worked too—she went about two notches down on the scary scale. She was still totally intimidating though.

By the time she returned her attention to Léo, Ben was getting really nervous. It was not fun to be standing in the middle of a group and have no idea what was being said, especially when everyone else looked so apprehensive. The woman turned her head to look Ben up and down and said something. He would swear his hair started to sweat. Luckily, Léo jumped in with a reply, diverting her attention. With one final declaration, she turned and swept away.

They all slowly sank into their seats. Lucien grabbed his wineglass and took a healthy swig.

"Who was that?" Ben murmured, afraid to speak too loudly in case she heard him and came back, even though she was already out of the restaurant.

"Claudette Bernard," Léo said. "She's one of the reigning matriarchs of Paris society."

"And certainly the scariest," Malik added. "I'm not ashamed to say that if I could have hidden under the table without her knowing, I would have."

"I think we need another bottle." Lucien looked around, and their waiter appeared as if by magic. That was one of the things Ben could appreciate about spending huge amounts of money for a meal—the service was impeccable. Or maybe that was because of the company he was in. The waiter fussed over their half-eaten meals, and Léo assured him it was nothing to do with the food. Which was true, because Ben's meat—Léo had made him take a bite before he told him it was hare—was amazing.

"What was she saying?" Ben decided he needed to know, even if he regretted it.

"Mostly to tell us we were a disgrace," Malik said gloomily. "There was also something about getting older and needing to settle down. None of us are even thirty yet, but she made me feel like a dirty old man."

"She asked about you too," Lucien put in, smiling at the sommelier so gratefully that the man looked worried as he opened the bottle and poured them more wine.

"Me?" Ben could actually feel the blood draining from his face.

"Don't worry," Léo said, but his attempt to reassure was in direct contrast to the expression on his face. "She just wanted to know who you were."

He wasn't reassured. "What did you tell her?"

Léo shrugged. "That you were visiting from Australia and didn't speak French. I didn't think she needed to know more than that."

Ben let out a shaky breath. "Who was that man with her?"

"Her son," Lucien said, finally looking a little steadier. "He brings her down here once a year for a week, probably to make up for the fact that he avoids her as much as possible for the rest of the year. We should order dessert."

"Cheese first," Malik insisted, and Lucien rolled his eyes.

"Of course. I would not dream of denying you cheese."

Ben perked up at that. One of his favorite things about Europe was the cheese.

A COUPLE OF HOURS LATER, Ben followed Léo into the apartment.

"Remind me to give you a key," Léo said as he dropped his in their usual spot on the sideboard. Warmth expanded in Ben's chest. A key. He was going to move in with Léo. Temporarily, of course, but still.

"Sure," he replied, then a pang of conscience made him add, "Are you sure about this?"

Léo stopped midway to the kitchen and turned to look at him. "You don't want to stay with me?"

Ben was shaking his head even before Léo had finished the sentence. "No, I do. I really do. Like, really." Now he felt like a dork again, but Léo was smiling, the smile that said he thought Ben was adorable, and his self-consciousness melted away.

"So, you want to stay with me, and I want you to…." Léo walked back toward him. "It seems that there isn't a problem, then. We'll get your things and check you out of the Fairmont tomorrow."

Ben's answer was lost in their kiss.

Chapter Ten

Two days later, with all of Ben's things in Léo's walk-in wardrobe and his final bill at the Fairmont settled (and the expression on his face when he'd seen it had made Léo want to take a picture), Léo and Ben were preparing dinner together. Ben had mentioned a craving for a "chicken parma," which Léo had at first refused to believe was a real thing. His description had sounded a little similar to chicken cordon bleu, so they had negotiated ingredients and agreed to try making a version they could both live with.

So far, it had been a messy undertaking. Ben had decided Léo should be in charge of dredging the chicken through the egg and then the breadcrumbs, and he'd been chewing on his lip when he'd suggested it, so somehow Léo had ended up with hands covered in gloppy—Ben's word —breadcrumbs while his laughing bunny snapped pictures.

That was when his phone rang. He glanced at the clock on the kitchen wall. Malik was at an auction for a collection of seventeenth-century firearms, and Léo had been expecting a call to tell him how much of Malik's funds needed to be moved from various investment accounts.

"Can you answer that?" he asked Ben, holding up his hands to indicate why he couldn't. "It's probably Malik."

Ben leaned over the bench and picked up Léo's phone. "It doesn't say Malik," he said as Léo went to the sink to wash his hands.

"It might still be him. Some of the auction houses don't allow private phones." He used his elbow to turn on the tap, and Ben raised the phone to his ear.

"Léo's phone," he said. There was a moment's pause, then, "This is Ben Adams. May I ask who's calling?"

Hell, it wasn't Malik after all. Léo grimaced, hoping it wasn't anyone too annoying. At least they spoke enough English to communicate with him.

"One moment please." Ben lowered the phone and turned panicked eyes on him. "Léo!" he hissed. "It's your father, and he does *not* sound happy!"

Léo slammed off the water and grabbed a dish towel, smearing it with the few breadcrumbs still on his hands as he strode across the kitchen. He tossed it aside and took his phone hastily.

"Hello, Father," he said in French, making an apologetic face at Ben, who held up his hands and shook his head, a pretty clear indication that Léo's father had been an ass.

"Léonard, what the hell are you up to? Your mother got a call yesterday from Claudette Bernard, who mentioned this little tourist you've apparently been playing around with. This morning André told me you also apparently took this boy to Carrere, and now he's answering your phone? What's wrong with you?"

Léo headed for the living room and the drinks cart. This was going to require fortification.

"Nothing's wrong with me, Father. I asked Ben to answer the phone because I was busy and I was expecting a call. I took him to Carrere because he needed a suit."

"Which he conned you into paying for, I'm sure," Charles Artois sneered. "You're letting some pretty back-packer take advantage of you."

"That is a terrible accusation." Léo poured gin into a tumbler with a heavy hand, looked at the tonic, then picked up the glass and took a sip. "I did not pay, in fact. He has money of his own. Not like us, but far more than he knows what to do with."

That gave his father pause. "That's not the impression I was given."

Léo avoided Ben's gaze as he paced across the living area. "Perhaps because your information comes from people who have neither met him nor spoken to me about him."

"So it is not true that you picked him up in the casino when he got drunk on champagne?" Léo winced. Who had his father been talking to?

"We met at the casino, yes, and shared a bottle of champagne and a meal," he extemporized. "I did not meet him 'when he was drunk.'"

Charles grumbled for a moment, words like "duty" and "responsibility" featuring heavily, and then, just as Léo was beginning to think the danger had passed, said, "Well, I suppose it doesn't matter too much. When does he leave?"

Léo looked at the ceiling and silently asked any deity who might be listening what he'd done to deserve this. He usually walked a fine line between doing as he pleased and not upsetting his father so much that his mother would call him and cry. Despite what many thought, he loved his parents and brother, and was extremely proud of his family heritage.

He just didn't want to be locked into eternal servitude to it.

"Actually," he finally said, "Ben has delayed departing for Italy while we take some time to get to know each other better. He's given up his hotel and is staying with me." There, that was all of it. Now his father had all the facts.

There was a long silence, so long that Léo began to wonder if maybe his father had passed out from shock. Should he—

"We will expect you on Friday," his father ordered. "Dinner is at eight o'clock."

Léo blinked. Did he mean Ben too? Because that was *not* a good idea.

"I beg your pardon, Fa—"

"Don't be late, Léo. Your mother is already distressed by all of this. If it gets out that you are living with someone we haven't even met, she will go into a decline." Léo was still shuddering at the thought of one of his mother's "declines" when Charles disconnected the call, leaving Léo standing with his phone to his ear. He lowered it slowly, wondering how he'd so completely lost control of the situation, and it rang again. A glance at the screen showed Malik's name.

"Hello?" he said.

"Don't worry about moving funds. There wasn't anything that would add to my collection," his cousin told him.

"My father just called."

Malik swore, which was unusual. He, like Léo, had been taught disdain for crude language from a young age. "Let me guess, Claudette Bernard told him about Ben."

"Among others," Léo agreed. "We've been summoned for dinner Friday night."

Malik hesitated. "By 'we,' you mean—"

"Me and Ben," Léo said dryly, a thread of humor rising.

"Oh." Malik's relief was clear. "I'd offer to come along as a distraction, but… well, I don't want to."

Léo couldn't help it; he laughed. "Thank you."

"You know I'd do anything for you. Just not that. What does Ben have to say about it?"

"He doesn't know yet. I had literally just hung up with Father when you called."

"Léo, does he know you were talking to your father?"

"Ye— Hell." Léo spun around to see Ben watching him, still a little pale, his concerned expression easing a little when Léo locked eyes with him. Damn, he'd been speaking in French the whole time. "Malik, I'll talk to you later." He disconnected the call before his cousin could reply, then tossed the phone onto the couch and knocked back the rest of the gin before putting the glass onto the coffee table. "I'm sorry, I forgot you couldn't understand. Was my father completely terrible to you?"

Ben shook his head and came to wrap his arms around Léo's waist. "He was… arrogant. Abrupt. But he didn't say anything rude." He rested his head against Léo's shoulder. "I take it he was not as nice to you?"

Léo took a deep breath, drawing in the scent of Ben's hair and taking comfort from the feel of him in his arms. It had been so easy to adjust to having Ben in his life; his easygoing humor, his keen intelligence, his down-to-earth practicality—just the thought of him leaving pained Léo.

"We need to go to Paris."

His bunny stiffened. "What? Why?" He drew back, but Léo refused to let him go entirely.

"My parents have heard that you moved in," he said, deciding not to mention he'd been the one to tell them, "and they'd like to meet you."

Ben's Adam's apple bobbed. "Léo, that's—"

"It will be fine," he interrupted, trying to sound soothing and nonchalant at the same time. "We will fly up on Friday afternoon, have dinner with them—a few hours at the most—then perhaps spend the weekend in Paris? Lucien would be delighted to see us. Or we can fly back on Saturday if you prefer." He smiled, radiating reassurance and innocence as hard as he could. Ben didn't look convinced.

"Léo, they're not likely to be happy about... us, are they?"

He sighed and let Ben go, taking his hand instead and pulling him down to sit on the couch. "They're not going to be unhappy, exactly. If my parents had had their way, I would have married the daughter of one of my father's business acquaintances when I was twenty-one. It would have been mutually beneficial for both families, and, according to my mother, for me and the girl as well. Once I'd made it very clear that my preference for men was not an experiment or a rebellious phase, they began considering possible alliances with families that had gay sons."

"Are you kidding?" Ben demanded incredulously, and Léo shook his head.

"Not at all. They would be happier if I married a woman, but their main priority was ensuring I married someone who would add to their social and financial clout."

"Wow. I mean, wow."

Léo chuckled. "Indeed. So I told them very emphatically that I would choose my own husband if and when I was ready to get married, and that if they wanted me to be part of their lives in any way, they would accept that. They actually do love me, and so we live in an uneasy détente. I spend most of my time in Monaco, doing as I please, and when I come to Paris, we carefully avoid speaking of my choices not to work in the family corporation or marry 'appropriately.' Well, my father sometimes slips and rants about my responsibility to put my education and abilities to good use, and if I attend a party where my mother has had influence on the guest list, there will always be an oddly high number of young single gay men from suitable families. But otherwise, they are careful not to do anything that may make me walk away forever. In return, I visit them several times a year in addition to the traditional holidays, always answer when my mother phones, and oversee their personal finances myself."

"Okay, so the system… kind of works, but now you've got me living with you. And I don't think I meet your parents' idea of appropriate. So isn't that going to rock the boat? Won't they be upset?"

Relaxing back into the couch, Léo squeezed Ben's hand, and twined their fingers so it couldn't be easily pulled away. "It's possible," he admitted. "I think they always held hope that I would ultimately decide to settle down with someone of their choosing, that I just needed time to come to that decision. However, you are charming and personable, you will be a guest in their home, and they will hopefully be unwilling to anger me, so they will be on their best behavior. This dinner is mostly because they don't want people to find out their son is living with a man they haven't met."

Ben sighed heavily. "Fine. Okay. Sure. I can do this. Do *not* let me drink too much." Léo laughed, and Ben yanked fruitlessly at his hand. "I mean it, Léo. You've heard me when I get drunk. I can't embarrass myself like that in front of your parents."

Léo lifted their hands to his lips and kissed Ben's fingers. "I will be on guard," he promised, and Ben flopped back beside him on the couch.

"Then we'll do it." He squirmed a little, reaching beneath himself and producing Léo's phone. "Oh, did I hear you say Malik's name?"

Taking the phone, Léo nodded. "Yes, he phoned right after my father. He said he'd offer to come with us, but he doesn't want to."

Ben laughed, and Léo smiled too.

"Well, at least he's honest," Ben conceded.

Léo made a face. "It's actually a bit more complicated than that. He doesn't want my mother to associate him with marriage in any way, because she might start thinking again that he should marry. Then she'll talk to her sister, Malik's mother, and the pressure he is already getting from his father will multiply."

"Malik's father is putting pressure on him?" His bunny frowned, his tender heart clearly not liking that.

"Malik's father has very definite ideas of what Malik should be doing at this stage of his life, and Malik isn't doing any of them. He hasn't been home to visit for over five years because he simply cannot bear his mother's tears when he and his father argue. He has two brothers and five sisters he misses very much, and they don't often visit Europe. It's a difficult situation."

"Poor Malik," Ben commiserated. "At least he has you right here, and Lucien when he can get away from Paris."

"True. Now…." Léo stood and pulled Ben up with him. "If we don't finish with that chicken, we won't eat until midnight."

After dinner had been cooked, eaten, and cleaned up, Léo excused himself to call Jean and organize their travel arrangements. They had decided to stay in Paris Saturday night too and fly back after brunch on Sunday morning. That would give them time to see Lucien, and for Léo to show Ben "another side of Paris." Since Ben had a feeling that included all the expensive shops and restaurants he'd avoided on his previous visit there, he had mixed feelings about it.

He poured himself some port and took it out onto the balcony. Even though the sun had long since gone down and there was no moon, it was beautiful—and peaceful. The ocean sang less than a hundred meters away, and the warm summer breeze was laden with the heady scent of flowers. He checked his watch and decided it was late enough to call.

Dani picked up on the second ring. "Hey, everything okay? You don't normally call at this time. Domestic bliss getting you down already?"

Ben grinned, feeling so much more positive just for having heard her voice. "Did I wake you?"

"Nah, I'm just out of the shower. Talk to me while I get dressed and make myself look like a corporate drone." He could hear her rummaging, probably through her cosmetics. She didn't wear a lot of makeup but her "work face" was a necessity.

"Sure. Wanna hear some drama?"

"Ooh, drama! Of course."

"Léo's dad called earlier, because he heard I'm living with Léo, and we've basically been ordered to go to Paris and have dinner with them Friday." He went on to fill her in on the background Léo had told him, interrupted by her frequent sarcastic comments.

"Wow," she said when he finished. "That's… wow."

"Yep." From the background sounds, it seemed like she was on her way out to her car. "Do you need to go?"

"Not just yet, but soon. Quickly, tell me what you know about Léo's family."

"Not much. What you told me. Generations old, dad and brother in many businesses, mum a princess. Oh, but I did hear that his sister-in-law is pregnant. Until then, I didn't even know he had a sister-in-law."

"Okay, here's what we'll do. If you can without upsetting Léo, check out his Wikipedia page. There's some info on there about the family. I think the dad and brother have pages too, but not as detailed. I'll see what else I can find. You can't walk into this unprepared. And ask Léo what you need to wear to dinner. Yeah?"

Ben sighed, but in reality the sense of relief was overwhelming. "Yeah. Thanks, Dani."

"Anytime. Talk later." And she was gone.

THEY FLEW to Paris from Nice in a private plane. The original plan had been to take a helicopter from Monaco to Nice, but Léo had decided at the last minute that he wanted to drive. Not the Veyron, of course—he would never leave his baby sitting at an airport for days, not even under the watchful eyes of the valets. No, instead he brought out the Aston Martin Vanquish, another car Ben would have been afraid to wear shoes in just a few short weeks ago.

Wow, his life really was changing.

The plane, for example. He'd always figured private

planes were just smaller. He hadn't realized that they could be kitted out so luxuriously, with an actual bedroom and full shower room, a kitchenette, and sofas, chairs, and tables. He had full Wi-Fi connectivity, access to a range of entertainment, and of course an attendant just waiting to fulfill his every wish.

The pilot had come back and greeted them personally, welcoming Léo aboard and introducing himself to Ben. Apparently the plane belonged to the Artois family personally, not the corporation. That's right, it wasn't used for business travel at all, just for things like skiing weekends in Switzerland or a shopping jaunt in Milan. You know, the usual.

Of course, it was a short flight, so Ben didn't feel he really had time to appreciate the advantages of the plane. He'd flown business class from Australia to London—he could have afforded first class, but despite the urge to splurge couldn't bring himself to spend that kind of money on a flight—so this kind of luxury in the air was amazing to him.

Léo's assistant, Jean, met them at the airport with a chauffeur-driven car. "I hope you don't mind," Léo had said when explaining the plans to Ben. "There are a few things we need to go over, and if we do it in the car, the rest of my time will be free to spend with you." Ben hadn't been bothered in the slightest, and was even less so when he realized the "car" was in fact a fully stocked limo, complete with wet bar. It was weird; he was constantly aware of the money in Léo's life, but Léo treated it so casually that it kind of faded on a day-to-day basis. He was a guy who lived in an apartment and drove a car and went out with friends to local businesses. And then there would be something like the suit, or the preferential treatment he received at restaurants, or the plane, and Ben would be reminded that Léo's level of rich was beyond what most people could even conceive of.

He sat back now and studied his lover. Léo's gorgeous dark looks mesmerized him, as always, but there were many hot men in the world. It was Léo's presence that Ben found truly captivating, just as he had that first night in the Place du Casino.

His gaze slid sideways to Jean. Léo's assistant, currently taking notes as Léo made comments about the document he was reading, was a tall, fit man in his early twenties. He'd greeted them with a tablet in one hand and a sheaf of papers in the other, and everything since that moment had been ruthlessly organized. Ben thought that if he ever had need of an assistant, he'd want one less... exacting. Because Jean made him feel vaguely incompetent. In the best possible way, of course.

By the time the car stopped at the destination, Ben had dreamed up several things he could make his imaginary assistant do just for the hell of it. He got out and looked around. Every building had a doorman, and there were no gawking tourists or low-budget cars on the street. He had a feeling that when he found out the name of the street and told Dani, she'd be able to give him reams of information about the wealthy magnates and celebrities who lived there. He was intensely glad they were staying at Léo's place and not going directly to the family home.

"Come." Léo took his hand and led him into the building as the doorman rushed forward to help with their overnight bags.

AT 7:27 THAT EVENING, Ben stood with Léo in front of a gorgeous building in the seventh arrondissement. Léo had told him the house had been in the family since the seventeenth century, which was part of why Ben was now clinging to Léo's hand in an attempt not to flee. He was wearing his new suit but had a feeling he'd still feel underdressed when they got inside.

He took a deep breath. "Okay, I'm ready," he announced.

Léo turned his head to meet his gaze. "I don't think I am," he confessed, and Ben's jaw dropped.

"Really?"

"I am worried they will behave badly, or otherwise convince you I am not worth your time."

Ben laughed, because really… Léo, not worth his time? As if. "Come on. We're both going to dread this until it's done." He tugged on Léo's hand until they'd reached the front door. Léo muttered something and rang the bell.

"Remind me, if dinner's at eight, why are we here at seven thirty?"

"Drinks," Léo muttered. "They never sit down to dinner without drinks first."

"Of course," Ben said. "Hey, that might help. Just remember, you promised not to let me get drunk."

Léo was smiling when the door opened. The middle-aged man there was wearing an immaculate suit, and Ben wondered if maybe there would be other guests at dinner.

"Good evening, Monsieur Artois," the man said. "Monsieur Adams. The family is in the west salon."

"Thank you, François," Léo said as they entered. "Do not bother to announce us." The man's mouth opened to say something, but Léo was already sweeping Ben along the corridor, so quickly he only had a vague impression of high ceilings and ornate plasterwork.

"Who was that?" he asked as they hurried up a staircase. "How come he was speaking English?"

"Butler," Léo said shortly. "And believe me when I tell you, my parents know much more about you than just that you don't speak French."

On that reassuring note, he stopped in front of a door and threw it open. The four people in the room turned to look as they entered.

Ben was suddenly incredibly aware that he'd bought his underwear three-for-five dollars at his local supermarket.

Léo's father stood and strode toward them. He was somewhere in his sixties, most of his hair still midbrown, although the gray was definitely stepping up its efforts. His eyes were gray too, his skin much paler than Léo's dusky bronze. From the looks of it, his suit had been made by Carrere or his Parisian brother. His face was set in a faintly disapproving frown.

"Léo. Where is François?"

"We outpaced him," Léo said, and his voice was different. Even that first night in Monaco, when Ben had thought him so arrogant, when his voice had dripped with disdain, there had been... something there, something softer. Warmer. Now, he was cold. As he leaned forward to kiss his father on both cheeks, a shiver ran down Ben's spine. He really didn't want to spend this evening with Léo the robot and his cold family. "Father, this is Benedict Adams. Ben, my father, Charles Artois."

Ben offered his hand. "Good evening, Monsieur Artois." Charles Artois nodded curtly and shook his hand briefly. Ben considered that good enough and went willingly when Léo took his arm and guided him to where two women sat on a sofa. Léo bent and kissed the older one.

"Mother," he greeted, and then he kissed the younger woman. "Ben, my mother, Myriam, and my sister-in-law, Celine."

Ben inclined his head politely. "Thank you for inviting

me this evening," he said, and when Myriam Artois offered her hand, he took it and bent over it awkwardly. She wasn't holding it like she wanted him to shake it, but he didn't feel confident enough to kiss it. He hoped he wasn't already making an arse of himself. Truthfully, he was almost more intimidated by the small stature and dark beauty of Léo's mother than he was by the arrogance of Léo's father.

Celine was a classically lovely blue-eyed blonde with a baby bump and a friendly smile. "It is nice to meet you," she said, her accent quite heavy. "I am happy to be practicing my English." Ben smiled back at her, trying not to grin unrestrainedly in relief. He felt like maybe he should congratulate her on her pregnancy, but didn't want to say anything in case… he wasn't sure what.

Finally, they moved to the last person in the room, a tall man standing by the window. Ben was slightly taken aback to realize the view from the window was of the Eiffel Tower—and it was *close*. He dragged his gaze away and focused on Léo's brother. It could be nobody else; the likeness was quite startling. Gabriel was perhaps a little heavier, with silver beginning to thread his hair, and the shape of his face was more their father's, but otherwise, Ben wouldn't have been surprised if they'd been taken for twins as children.

"Ben, so pleased to meet you," Gabriel said, reaching out to shake Ben's hand while slinging his other arm around Léo's shoulders and dragging him close.

"I'm pleased to meet you too," Ben blurted, shaking his hand heartily and smiling. "*So* pleased." Léo smiled faintly at that, and Ben's courage was bolstered enough for him to say, "Congratulations, by the way."

Gabriel grinned. "Thank you." He glanced over Ben's shoulder. "Shall we have drinks?"

The next few minutes passed in a flurry of settling into

chairs as drinks were concocted and passed around. Ben was torn between wanting to join Celine in a sparkling water, thus ensuring he couldn't get drunk and say something stupid, and desperately needing the numbing effect of alcohol as Léo's mother continued to watch him with a carefully neutral expression.

To say that conversation was stilted was a laughable understatement. Gabriel asked Ben about his travels, but Ben was so self-conscious, he found himself stammering, his face getting hotter and hotter. Finally Léo laid a hand over his and squeezed, then interrupted to ask Celine how her parents were. This led to a description of the renovations on her parents' home and a discussion of the chaos of renovating in general, and Ben remained gratefully silent.

By the time they were seated for dinner in the incredibly elegant "family" dining room, Ben was feeling a little more in control. He'd had enough to drink that his nerves had settled, but not so much that he was in danger of blurting out the details of his and Léo's sex life.

He hoped.

"You have a lovely home, madame," he said to Léo's mother. It was absolutely true, but also an attempt to get on her good side.

She inclined her head. "Thank you."

Ben tried not to wince. Clearly she wasn't interested in conversing with him.

"Ben, what work do you do?" Charles Artois asked, although "demanded" was probably more accurate. Ben had always thought Léo arrogant, but compared to his father, he was positively self-effacing.

"I'm a nurse," he said. "I specialize in home healthcare for the terminally ill."

"That must be very difficult," Celine offered sympathetically. "If they are terminally ill, you cannot make them well again."

Ben nodded. "It can be hard, but knowing they're able to stay in their homes and be comfortable is some consolation. A lot of people can't stand the idea of a nursing home or hospice care."

"They die with some dignity," Léo's father declared, and Ben blinked at the almost approval in his voice. "It is good that you can help them."

From the way Léo's fork clanged against his plate, he was just as surprised as Ben. The status quo returned a moment later though.

"When must you return to your... job?" Myriam asked. Considering that Léo had told him Charles worked a ridiculous number of hours per week, Ben wasn't sure why she'd infused "job" with such disdain. Perhaps working was only allowed when you owned the company?

"There is no set date, madame," he said politely. "When I return to Australia and am ready to work again, I'll let the agency know, and they'll find a client for me."

"And when will you be returning to Australia?" Myriam again, not even trying to hide the intent behind the question. *When can I get you out of my son's life?*

"I don't have a set date," Ben repeated uncomfortably.

"Ben and I are spending time together," Léo said firmly. "I don't want him to go back to Australia just yet."

"He has plenty more of Europe to see, in any case," Gabriel added smoothly, in an obvious attempt to divert conversation. "I'm sure he won't be returning home for some time."

"But surely his family misses him," Myriam said. Ben felt a pang of guilt, because his mum had said she missed him the last time they spoke. He should probably call her more often.

"He speaks to his family regularly," Léo interjected. "More often than I speak to you." *Or will in the future*, his tone implied. Myriam froze, then returned her attention to her plate.

Crap, crap, crap, Ben thought. He reached for his wineglass, took a gulp of the really excellent red wine, then set the glass down carefully beside his plate.

And threw caution to the wind.

"Madame, monsieur, I'm aware that I'm not your ideal mate for Léo. I regret that this is the case. It would make things much easier if my presence in your son's life thrilled you. You could be happy, Léo and I could be happy, and you would maybe develop a better relationship with Léo. We could visit every month, and I would call you Mum and Dad—or maybe not," he added as Gabriel choked on his wine. "But anyway"—fuck, why wasn't Léo stopping him?—"um, anyway, that's not how things are. Life is not a fairy tale. Well, when I met Léo it was kind of like a fairy tale. Except I thought he was going to assassinate me." Gabriel moaned, and Léo sat frozen at Ben's side. "The point is… the point is, things don't always go the way you want. Léo and I are spending time together. Whether it goes further than that is yet to be seen. Whether you're a part of his life is entirely dependent on your own behavior. Family is not optional, and that means we need to make allowances for what we think are stupid choices, so you need to make allowances for me, because I'm Léo's stupid choice." He snatched up his wineglass and knocked back the remaining contents, then held the glass out to Léo. "More, please."

Wordlessly, Léo obliged. And then, as Ben sipped slightly more decorously, they all sat in frigid silence.

Great. He'd made it *worse*.

"You thought Léo was going to *assassinate* you?"

Charles burst out. "What about my son could possibly resemble an assassin?"

"That's exactly what I thought!" Léo exclaimed.

"It wasn't like that." Ben wished he'd kept his mouth shut. The thinly veiled hints that he should leave the continent hadn't been that bad.

"It sounds like a fascinating story," Celine said. "Will you tell it to us?" She was so pretty and so earnest, and her smile was genuinely friendly, and Ben could not resist. He found himself telling her—well, everyone, really, but mostly her—about how Léo had introduced him to glorious champagne and fine dining and romanced him with drinks on a moonlit terrace, then kissed him by a floodlit rooftop pool and left him to chaste dreams. He compared it all to a movie, and related his fear that it was too good to be true, and how the assassination theory came about.

"What happened next?" Myriam asked eagerly. "How did he prove he was genuine?"

Ben swallowed a gasp. Who would have thought Léo's mother was a romantic?

"Er... he took me to lunch, and then we spent the afternoon at the Musée océanographique."

"He willingly went to an aquarium?" Charles shook his head admiringly. "Well, that would prove he was interested."

This is weird. Right? It was definitely weird. Ben shot Léo a pleading glance, but Léo seemed to be completely focused on his plate, a tiny smile curving his lips.

"Well, it is a lovely way to meet," Celine declared. "A story worth telling."

"Thanks," Ben said weakly. Too bad he felt like a complete idiot.

Surprisingly, though, it seemed to have broken the ice.

Although neither Charles nor Myriam were exactly friendly, they at least were polite and stopped asking pointed questions about his return to Australia. The conversation flowed more easily, mostly about people and events known to the family, and at one point Myriam interrupted herself to ensure Ben knew the backstory behind her anecdote, just as if he were a guest she actually wanted there.

By the time they'd finished coffee in the library—yes, an actual library, lined with book-filled shelves—the knots that had been strangling Ben's stomach were gone, and Léo was also far more relaxed. They left on a much more positive note than they'd arrived, with Celine informing Ben that she would be in Nice next month to visit a friend, and she would come to Monaco and have lunch with him. Ben smiled and nodded and wondered if it would be too weird for Dani to join them via his iPhone.

The journey back to Léo's apartment was quiet—mostly from exhaustion, Ben figured. It took a lot of energy to be that nervous, and he'd probably had more alcohol than he really should have. He'd been doing so well with the "drink often but never be drunk" thing too. Oh well. Some occasions called for a drunken stupor.

Inside, Ben took the opportunity to look around. He'd *seen* the apartment before dinner, of course, but hadn't appreciated it, what with the nerves. Now he took in what was by Paris standards a large space, impeccably decorated, of course—he'd expect nothing less of one of Léo's homes—and completely clean. There was not even a speck of dust on any surface.

"Why is it so clean in here?" he asked as Léo sank into an armchair.

Léo looked at him as if he were an imbecile. "Because the cleaner made certain of it."

"Oh. You called and told them we were coming? Lucky they could squeeze you in on such short notice." Ben wanted to kick off his shoes and curl up on the sofa, but there was no way he was doing that in his Carrere suit.

"She comes every week," Léo said, and Ben froze with one arm out of his jacket.

"But you don't live here," he said softly, and Léo sighed.

"No, but when I do come here, I don't want to battle foot-deep drifts of dust. Let it go, Ben, please."

Ben pulled his jacket the rest of the way off and carefully draped it over a chair, then crossed over to perch on the arm of Léo's armchair. "I'm sorry. I'm working on it. I swear I am."

With a swift tug, Léo pulled him into his lap. "There is nothing to work on. I'm just tired." They cuddled for a while, leaning their heads against each other and just basking in the warmth of each other's bodies.

"Tonight went pretty well," Ben finally said. "I mean, apart from me running my trap and sounding like an idiot. But at least your mum stopped dropping hints about me leaving. For a while I was afraid she might have me deported. Does she have any contacts with the—"

"I love you."

Ben was sure his heart stopped beating. "What?" he whispered.

Léo lifted his head and locked their gazes. "I love you. I love that you talk incessantly about foolish things. I love that you are kind and sweet. I love the way you look and the way you react to me in bed. I love—"

Ben stopped him with a kiss. It was meant to be quick, just a way of shutting him up so Ben could get a word in, but it lingered, drawing out and becoming something more. When they finally broke apart, he couldn't remember what he wanted to say.

"I love the way you dealt with my parents. I love that you're always secretly outraged when I use valet parking. I love everything about you."

"I love you too," Ben murmured. Then laughed. "Oh my God, this really is a fairy tale." He straightened, and somehow slid off Léo's lap, arms flailing, and landed hard on his arse. "Ow."

Léo looked down at him. "I love how clumsy you are."

Chapter Eleven

D espite Ben's stated desire to spend Saturday in bed, Léo had a plan, so he told Ben to get up so they could "explore Paris."

Of course, Ben insisted that he'd seen Paris, that he'd spent ten days in the city. Léo agreed that that was sufficient time to see the tourist highlights, and knowing Ben as he did, he imagined he and Dani had also googled "non-touristy things to do in Paris" and Ben had done all of those too. But then, "exploring Paris" was just an excuse to get Ben out of the apartment.

So they ate a leisurely breakfast of pastries and coffee at the patisserie two streets over, which had long been one of his favorites. Then Léo took Ben shopping.

He whined the whole way.

"Léo, I don't need anything. God knows you can't possibly need anything, you already own everything there is. Where are we going anyway? Are you going to make me shop for clothes? Because I swear, I've bought more clothes on this trip than I have in *years*."

"One thing I have noticed about you is that you mostly buy only the things you need. Don't you think you deserve to buy something frivolous just because you want it?" Léo tried to keep the amusement out of his voice as their driver pulled up at their destination.

"While the clothes I've bought lately can definitely be called frivolous purchases, I'd question whether I actually wanted them," Ben retorted. He followed Léo out of the car and crossed his arms. "Well? Where are we going?"

"Here," Léo said, and led him into the LEGO store. Ben gazed around, mouth slightly open, then pulled himself together.

"You know, I can buy LEGO in Australia."

"Not all the sets are available there. I checked. I remembered you saying you used to love playing with LEGO as a boy, but that it was so expensive you didn't get much."

Ben's face softened. "Yeah. Mum and Dad used to buy little sets for me for birthdays and Christmas." He looked around again, this time with a big grin. "I can't believe you thought of this. This is *awesome*." He paused. "Although, I think I'd feel a bit silly buying some of this."

Léo smiled, glad he'd guessed correctly. "Ah, but there is a grown-up way to do this." He grabbed Ben's hand and guided him across the store to where the Architecture kits were. He'd spent quite a bit of time online researching exactly what he wanted, and he'd done it all himself instead of delegating anything to Jean, right down to calling the store and ensuring they had the desired items in stock. "I thought," he began, "that you could use this as a way of commemorating your travels." He gestured to the display. Before them was a cityscape of London, complete with the Eye and the Tower Bridge. Not far away were kits for Big Ben and Buckingham Palace, and on the shelf below were the Louvre and the Eiffel Tower. "Obviously they don't have sets for everywhere you've been, but—"

He was cut off by Ben's enthusiastic hug. "You're the *best*, Léo! This is the best shopping trip I've ever been on!"

Léo watched smugly as his bunny began grabbing sets, chattering about which one he was going to construct first. He was pretty sure he'd be called on to assist, but even that couldn't dispel the warm glow. Never had anyone responded so enthusiastically to such a simple and inexpensive gift. He'd gotten less appreciation when he'd taken his boyfriend of several years ago to follow the Grand Prix circuit for six months.

Once he'd selected the Architecture kits he wanted, Ben decided it wasn't that big a deal for adults to have LEGO, and began browsing through the Star Wars selection. Léo watched in amusement, taking things when he was instructed to and then quickly passing them off to the delighted hovering sales assistant.

After that, he took Ben to Ladurée. It was not one of his usual haunts, but from their table by the window, he could point out the few local patrons among the tourists, and also those contemporaries of his parents walking by on the street. Early Saturday afternoon was the time to see and be seen, and Léo kept Ben in quiet fits of giggles as he related gossip and stories that the subjects would no doubt wish had been forgotten. Ben was so preoccupied that he almost didn't react to the cost of their coffee and macarons.

Then he whisked Ben back to the apartment and made love to him. Perhaps it was something they could "do anywhere," but Léo didn't care, and Ben didn't seem to, either.

THAT EVENING, they met Lucien at Epicure.

"Is this one of your favorite restaurants?" Ben asked, glancing around. They were seated at their table but still waiting for Lucien and his date.

"No," Léo said. "It's a good restaurant, but we're here because Lucien's date wanted to come, and since he insisted they eat with us, it seemed fair to concede the location."

"We're crashing Lucien's date?" Ben sounded something between horrified and amused.

Léo shrugged. "Lucien prefers the company of friends to casual dates. He didn't want to be rude, so he offered the option of joining us."

"Or he'd break the date?"

Léo nodded. "Most likely." He gestured toward the door. "Here they are." Ben turned his head to look and gasped.

"Léo, that's a woman."

Léo considered the various possible responses to what was really a ridiculous statement, and went with the simplest. "Yes, I know."

"But I thought Lucien was gay!" Ben hissed, and Léo suddenly understood.

"No, Lucien's sexuality is quite fluid. He's not fixated on either gender."

"He's bi?"

"I suppose." Léo hadn't thought about Lucien's preferences for a long time. Basically, his friend looked for attractive, confident, and willing. Anything else was negotiable.

Lucien and the stunning brunette woman reached their table, and Léo and Ben stood for introductions. The woman, Denise, seemed friendly enough, but as they sat and began to peruse their menus, he noticed that she kept slipping into French, even though they'd advised her Ben only spoke English.

At first, he thought perhaps she was not confident in her ability to speak English, but as Ben enthusiastically described their trip to the LEGO store, she seemed to follow the conversation well enough, making several comments that were... not rude, exactly. They were clever and only mildly sarcastic, but where she tried to pass them off as jokes, Léo soon became convinced they were not. More, whenever she wasn't speaking directly to Ben, she defaulted to French, essentially excluding him. Ben said nothing, but Léo noticed his withdrawal as the meal progressed.

Lucien seemed to notice too. Halfway through their main course, when Denise began an anecdote—in French—he leaned toward her and murmured something. Denise pasted an obviously fake surprised expression on her face and looked at Ben.

"Ben, I'm so sorry. I keep forgetting that not everyone is fortunate enough to be educated in a second language."

Léo put down his knife and fork, but Lucien beat him to it. Standing abruptly, he drew back Denise's chair.

The waiter hurried toward them, but Lucien waved him off as Denise exclaimed in surprise. "Lucien, what are you doing?"

"You're leaving," he announced. "I'll have the maître d'hotel arrange a taxi for you. I regret that I cannot escort you home."

As Denise protested, demanding to know *why*, and doing so loudly enough to attract the attention of other diners (Léo's mother would have been disgusted), Lucien took her arm and "helped" her from her chair.

"Your discourtesy to Ben has been most obvious, Denise, and since I would much rather spend the evening in the company of my friends than with a woman who cannot even be polite, that is what I will do."

While Lucien had rather pointedly spoken in English, Denise's reply was in loud French.

"He is just a foolish, low-class tourist. How you even thought to subject me to his company on what was supposed to be our evening together—" She was cut off as Lucien hustled her away.

Léo reached out and took Ben's hand. His bunny was staring at his plate, face flushed bright red. For the first time in his life, Léo wanted to cause a public scene. He wished he'd spoken before Lucien had, wished he'd put that vile woman in her place. More, he wished his mother had been there to slice the bitch to ribbons with a quiet comment and a dismissive look.

"I regret that our day was spoiled by that woman," he said quietly, and Ben looked up.

"It wasn't spoiled," he declared. "Nothing could spoil this day. And, if anything, it was kind of nice to have Lucien stick up for me so forcefully." He made a face. "I should probably try to learn French, though."

Lucien returned in time to hear that. "Ben, I apologize most sincerely for subjecting you to that woman," he said. "I, for one, have been glad to have the chance to practice my English."

Ben chuckled, and the fist around Léo's heart loosened. "Lucien, that's sweet, but if I'm going to hang around for a while, it's not a bad idea to learn the local language."

"In that case, it would be my pleasure to assist you," Lucien offered promptly.

"I'll help him," Léo said repressively, not really sure where the wisp of jealousy had come from. He knew

Lucien would never poach, and he trusted Ben implicitly. Love was just not rational. In an attempt to cover up his foolishness, he added, "Now, let us tell you about dinner with my parents last night."

Chapter Twelve

"I can't believe you're meeting all these people," Dani whined as Ben sat on the balcony at Léo's apartment with a glass of really amazing wine, and alternated between looking at her and gazing out over the Mediterranean. He had his phone propped against the wine bottle so she could see him and they could talk "face-to-face." "It's ridiculous," she continued. "You don't even care about celebrities, and here you are, meeting the rich and famous at parties and actually *talking* to them."

"You don't care about celebrities either," Ben reminded her, then sipped from his glass and sighed contentedly. He remembered with vague fondness the days—just months ago—when he'd cheerfully bought two-dollar bottles of wine and called it good enough. Now that he was used to drinking "real" wine, as Léo called it, there was no way he could ever go back. Dani had laughed when he'd told her that, but he'd shipped her a case of his new favorite red, and she'd called at three in the morning to rhapsodize over it, swearing to never drink anything else. He hadn't told her how much it cost because he was pretty sure that would ruin her pleasure.

Dani made a face. "No, but if I had the opportunity to meet them, I'd at least learn all about them first. Not like you, who had to be told the next day by your best friend exactly who you'd met." She sipped from her own wineglass and smiled.

"That only happened once," Ben protested. "And he wasn't exactly an A-list celebrity."

"I knew who he was," Dani said smugly. Ben narrowed his eyes.

"About that," he said. "I've been thinking. You have no interest in polo. In fact, you barely have an interest in sports that are popular in Australia, much less something like polo. How did you know the identity of a Spanish polo player?" She smirked, and his suspicions were confirmed. "You cheat!"

"How is it cheating?" she asked through her laughter. "You told me you were going to a specific party. I just did a Google search to see if there was any info out there and got really lucky that the article about the party was published about two minutes before you called me. You weren't mentioned in that article, by the way."

Ben tried to sulk but couldn't hold back his chuckle. "It's been killing me, not knowing how you did it."

"Well, now you know." She leaned back in her armchair and had some more wine. The glass was now only a third full. Soon, she'd be off to bed. "So, where's Léo this afternoon? Waiting impatiently again?"

Ben shook his head. "Malik decided he wanted a new car, so they've been shopping all day. I think it's one of the few types of shopping Léo likes to do himself."

"What's wrong with Malik's car?" Dani asked. Ben

leveled a stare at the screen of his phone, and she groaned. "He's just buying a car for the hell of it?"

"Pretty much. His favorite until the day before yesterday was a Ferrari, I think. That's the one with the horse emblem, right?"

Dani nodded.

"Yeah, so he's been in love with his Ferrari, but now he's thinking it's time for a change. He's not sure exactly what he wants next, so they're going to test drive a bunch of different cars that I've never heard of. I kid you not, that's exactly how the conversation went."

"Why didn't you go shopping with them?"

Ben shrugged. "I really wanted to, but then I would have missed our call," he said. There was a moment's pause, and then they both burst out laughing. "Oh my God, I can't believe I said that with a straight face!"

"Neither can I!" Dani gasped for breath. "I just asked because I wanted to see you spill your drink or something." Ben wiped a tear from his eye and sighed.

"So...." Dani's face screwed up with indecision.

"So?"

"So, have you and Léo talked about what happens next?"

Ben went cold.

"What do you mean?" He tried to keep his voice light, tried to pretend he hadn't spent the past few weeks not thinking about the need to have this conversation, both with her and Léo.

She sighed. "Don't play dumb, Benji. You've been in Monaco nearly four months, living with Léo for three of those. By now, you were supposed to have seen Italy, Switzerland, Austria, and Germany, and be on the verge of either heading farther north or coming home, depending on your mood. If being with Léo was making you happy, I'd be all for it, but you're nuts if you think I can't tell you're bored. I think you're entitled to talk to Léo about whether you should be applying for Monégasque citizenship and looking for some way to fill your day, or moving on."

His face got hot. "I'm not bored, exactly. And don't call me Benji."

"Then what are you, exactly? Originally, Léo was going to be a fling. You couldn't possibly be really attracted to him because he was idle rich, didn't have a job. Remember? Then you decided it was okay to spend a bit more time with him, because he's great and he gets you and you have fun together. But now it's been months, you know he's not a complete slacker *and* that he has a social conscience, and—to repeat—you've been living with him for months, doing nothing but going to parties and lazing around. That's great for some people, but I know you, Ben. When you learned the history of the Danish monarchy last week, that wasn't because you're actually interested in Danish history."

Ben pressed his lips tightly together and then huffed. "Fine," he admitted. "I was bored shitless. In fact, I was so bored that I asked Léo to tell me all about how he'd invested my money, but numbers have never been my strength, and my mind wandered after five minutes. He had an invitation on his desk from the Crown Prince of Denmark, and it just sort of snowballed from there. I've read every book I can lay hands on that interests me, some of them twice. Léo keeps me busy some of the time—okay, most of the time—but he works sometimes, or has stuff with Malik, or Lucien if he's here, and they always ask me, but sometimes they should have time just for them, right? I don't want to be a clingy boyfriend. And for the, I don't know, fifteen hours every week that I'm on my own, I have nothing left to do!" He sucked in a deep breath. "I looked online, and there are short-term and relief nursing jobs around, especially now that I'm learning French and have organized a long-stay visa, but I'd need to meet a bunch of conditions to get a work permit, and it's not worth the hassle if I'm just going to be leaving soon."

Dani pursed her lips. "Are you leaving soon?"

Ben knocked back the remainder of the wine in his glass. "I don't know," he said honestly. "The thought of leaving Léo makes my stomach hurt, but then I wonder if that's just part of the holiday lenses."

The what-the-fuck look on his best friend's face almost made him laugh. "Holiday lenses?"

"Yeah. You know, like rose-colored glasses, but specifically for places you see and people you meet while on holiday."

"You're worried that what you feel for Léo is just because you're in a glamorous place, and that if you settle into everyday life there, those feelings will go away." Dani's tone was so flat that Ben winced.

"It sounds dumb when you say it like that," he complained.

"It's not the way I said it that made it sound dumb," she told him. "Think about it, Ben. You just finished telling me you're so bored that you were willing to learn about investing and the history of the Danish royal family, both topics that have never interested you, and yet despite that, you don't want to leave and go to Italy, a place you've always dreamed of seeing."

Ben bit his lip.

"On top of that," she continued, now sounding so exasperated he almost expected her to reach through the phone and smack him upside the head, "you haven't just been seeing Léo occasionally. You've been living with him.

In his apartment. Sharing a bathroom, a kitchen, and all the rest. You spend most of your time with him. 'Familiarity breeds contempt' is a proverb for a reason, you know. I'll bet you've learned all his flaws, haven't you?"

"He doesn't have many," Ben protested, and she pounced.

"But he has some?"

"So do I!"

"I'm not saying you don't," she said with heavy-handed patience. "But when people first meet and they're in the la-la-love phase, they refuse to see each other's flaws. The fact that you see Léo's and still want to be with him means something."

Ben chewed on his lip, then stopped, remembering how much that turned Léo on. "You're right," he said finally. "But, Dani, if I stay... I'll miss you. Won't you miss me?"

"More than you can imagine," she said bluntly. "You'll have Léo to distract you, at least. But we can talk every day, if we want, and obviously I'll take every holiday I can in Europe. You guys can come visit here too. Your mum would probably have kittens if you never came home again."

Ben chuckled as she meant him to, but his mind was elsewhere, and when Dani finished her wine and wished him good night, he smiled and blew her kisses and wondered what the hell to do next.

Léo DROPPED his keys into their usual spot and called, "We're back," as he led Malik into the apartment.

"You sound so domesticated," his cousin commented, voice rife with amusement. Léo thought about taking exception to that, but decided he didn't care. He *was* rather domesticated these days, and he liked it. He loved knowing that he'd start and end each day with Ben.

So he smirked and raised an eyebrow at Malik. From the sour expression he got in return, his smugness had been noted.

"Hey," Ben said, coming down the corridor from the bedrooms. "How'd it go? Did you buy anything?" He leaned up to peck Léo on the mouth, but avoided eye contact, his attention mostly on Malik, and Léo's stomach dropped.

Don't be foolish, he chided himself. So Ben seemed a little distracted. Maybe he was just really interested in Malik's new car.

Even in his head that sounded stupid.

As his cousin waxed rhapsodic about his brand-new McLaren, and Ben pretended to be fascinated, Léo herded them into the living area and then headed for the drinks cart. He'd thought about installing a full wet bar, but had always found that to be a little tacky in a private home. He noted the open bottle of wine and guessed Ben had been chatting with Dani. Maybe he'd had bad news from home? Léo wished Malik would leave so he could ask.

He fetched them all drinks and settled on the couch as close to his bunny as he could. Ben didn't lean into him as he usually did, instead stiffening slightly. Malik must have noticed, because he stopped midsentence, umm'd for a moment, and then picked up again, shooting Léo a questioning look that Léo pretended he didn't see.

To Léo's everlasting gratitude, his cousin bolted down his drink and made excuses a few minutes later. Ben shot off the couch to show him out, which made Malik's jaw drop, because he'd been coming and going from Léo's homes for years without anyone bothering about such niceties. The look he gave Léo then was dire, with clear instructions to fix whatever the problem was.

"Lucien will be here on Friday night," he told Ben as they headed toward the front door. "He suggested we go to the roulette tournament at the casino and watch people throw money away on a fool's game. I think he wants to console one of the losers."

"Maybe," Léo heard Ben say, and he stood and began pacing. Ben had developed an odd fascination for Malik's and Lucien's dating lives, even going so far as picking out "likely" prospects for them if they were all out together. For him not to leap at this opportunity, something must definitely be wrong.

What the hell could it be? Everything had been going so well. Yes, he knew Ben was at somewhat of a loose end, but that was just because he wasn't used to not working. It wouldn't take long for him to become accustomed to it. Or maybe he could help Léo with some of his charity consulting. Not for investing, obviously, but a lot of charities concerned themselves with medical and health issues. A nurse advisor would be a big asset there. And now that the summer tourist season was well and truly over, Léo intended taking his bunny to Italy. He knew Ben had been looking forward to it, and planned to surprise him with the trip. They could spend several months there if they wanted, just wandering about. Léo quite liked the Italian countryside, as long as they avoided the tourists.

In the new year, he expected they'd be sorting out the paperwork for Ben's EU residency. Maybe planning a wedding. He wasn't particularly concerned about getting married himself, as long as he and Ben were together, but he knew his family would prefer a wedding, and if Ben wanted one, then he was in favor.

Ben came back into the room and collected the glasses

on the coffee table, and Léo wondered if he should talk to him about his thoughts for the future. He'd assumed they were on the same page, but maybe not.

Or Ben could be preoccupied for a different reason entirely.

His gaze lingering on the way Ben was chewing his lower lip, Léo decided to worry about it later. Ben would say something if he thought Léo needed to know, right?

He followed Ben into the kitchen, his intentions lascivious, and came up behind him at the sink, wrapping his arms around his bunny's waist.

"What do you think about the casino on Friday?" he asked, bending his head to kiss the soft spot beneath Ben's ear. "I think Lucien actually has his eye on one particular prospective loser." He tried to ignore the stiffness in Ben's body. "I've narrowed it down to—"

Ben turned in his arms and placed his hands on Léo's chest, but instead of caressing, he pushed slightly. Léo let him go and took a step back, alarm almost choking him.

"Léo, stop for a second. We need to talk about something."

Léo nodded, forcing himself to breathe normally even though he'd never heard of those particular words leading to anything good.

Ben looked around the kitchen, then took Léo's hand and led him back to the couch in the living room. He sat them both down and then stared fixedly at his hands, his breathing irregular. The urge to fix everything rose in Léo, and he stroked a finger over his bunny's cheek.

"Ben, whatever this is, we can fix it. I can help. Just tell me—"

Ben's strangled laugh cut him off. "Léo, I'm sorry," he began, and Léo's already strained nerves twanged. "I'm so sorry I'm freaking you out. Everything's fine. There's nothing to fix. I promise."

The air gushed out of Léo's lungs in relief, and he grabbed Ben and pulled him onto his lap. "You scared me," he muttered against his neck. "I was sure you were going to say that you were leaving, that you didn't love me."

Ben was shaking his head as he pulled Léo's face up and kissed him. "I love you," he said, then kissed him again. "I love you so much it shocks me. But I am leaving."

Léo went into freefall, his arms dropping nervelessly away from Ben as shock reverberated inside him. Distantly, he was aware that Ben was saying his name, but it didn't truly register amidst the explosive noise in his head.

Ben was leaving him.

Sharp pain brought him back to the living room. Ben had pinched him—hard. Léo gasped and yanked his arm away.

"Oh good, you're back. I'm sorry again. I blurted that out without thinking about how it would sound. Léo, I love you. I'm not leaving *you*."

Léo swallowed hard, the relief that flooded him battling with his fear and shock. Unable to sit still, he surged to his feet, remembering too late that Ben was in his lap. His bunny tumbled to the floor with a yelp.

"Je regrette," Léo muttered, helping him up but beginning to pace as soon as Ben was on his feet.

Ben grabbed his hand as he passed. "Léo, listen to me for a minute. I'm sorry I'm messing this up, but please try to hear me out."

Léo pulled his hand away and went to sit in the armchair across from the couch, afraid to touch Ben for fear he'd grab on and not let go.

Ben stood wringing his hands for a moment longer,

then slowly sat again and took a deep breath. "I love you," he started. "You know that, right?"

Léo nodded jerkily, not trusting himself to speak.

"Right, okay. So I'm not leaving you. But I am going to leave. I... I've been... a bit bored lately. I'm used to being busy all the time. Even when I was traveling through Europe, I packed every day with sightseeing and other activities. Being... idle has been difficult for me. I wanted to be with you, so I've been ignoring it, pretending it's okay, but I'm worried that it will become a problem between us."

Léo found his voice. "So we find something to occupy you. Leaving is going to be just as big a problem between us because we won't be together!"

Ben sighed. "I'm not leaving because of that. I'm sorry, I'm still fucking this up. I'm such a dipshit. Our time together has been amazing. Being with you is like a fairy tale. I love you so much, it hurts to think of being apart. But I've heard so many stories of holiday romances that just... fade away. And I'm scared that we'll settle into happiness here and I'll make huge changes in my life, and then in a couple of months it will turn out that it was just the holiday glow that made it so good."

That logic went through Léo's head a few times, but the flaws were still there. He shook his head, confused. "That doesn't make sense, Ben. You've just finished telling me you've been bored. If you were still seeing everything with 'holiday glow,' then you wouldn't have been bored. The fact that you could be at all dissatisfied means you're seeing things clearly."

"That's what Dani said." Ben rubbed his forehead. "But I can't help worrying. So I'm going to leave."

"Stop saying that!" Léo roared, his nerves frayed.

"But I'm coming back," Ben rushed to assure him.

"I'm going to continue my trip. I'm going to take the same amount of time I've spent here and see more of Europe. We'll stay in touch the whole time—phone calls, texts, maybe even the occasional overnight visit. But not being together all the time will give us space to assess if we're really meant to be together. If the feelings don't fade once we're not spending every second together, then I'll know I'm making the right decision to… move here. If that's what you want. And if they do start to fade, then it won't matter. We'll both remember our time together fondly but move on with our lives."

Léo waited for a three-count, wanting to make sure Ben was finished this time. When the silence began to draw out, he stood and went over to the drinks cart. His hand hovered as he tried to pick a drink, but nothing seemed quite right. In the end, he grabbed the vodka, glanced at the glasses, then took a belt straight from the bottle. He turned with the bottle still in hand to see Ben staring at him with his mouth open.

"Did you just drink from the bottle?" he asked faintly.

Léo ignored the question. "That is the stupidest idea anyone has ever come up with," he declared, hearing the rough edge to his voice and deciding more vodka was the answer. Ben's eyes followed the bottle's path and widened when Léo swallowed another slug. The liquor burned down his throat and dulled some of the turmoil inside him. He watched Ben's Adam's apple bob.

"It's not stupid," he defended.

"It fucking is!" Léo shouted. He whirled around and put the vodka back before he was tempted to throw it. When he turned back, Ben's face was sheet white.

"You swore," he said, his voice cracking. "You never swear."

Léo sucked in a deep, shaky breath through his nose,

fighting for control. He went over and sat next to Ben and took his hands.

"Listen to me," he urged, aware that his accent had deepened and struggling to keep his English vocabulary. "I love you. You're right, I never swear, but the thought of you leaving, even overnight, much less for months, makes me want to swear nonstop all day."

"And drink from the bottle," Ben added, smiling weakly.

"And drink from the bottle," Léo affirmed. "I'd even drink cheap wine." Ben chuckled, and Léo squeezed his hands. "You've made me so angry right now by suggesting that what we feel might not be real, that I know it is. It must be. How can I still love you while I'm this angry if it's not real?"

Ben swallowed again, his gaze dropping. "I guess that's true," he said, and hope surged in Léo.

"So you can see why your idea seems stupid to me," he went on. "Even though everything between us has been wonderful, there have been moments that were not perfect. If our feelings were going to fade, they would have started to do so in those moments. Yes?"

The silence pressed down between them, and a bead of sweat rolled down's Léo's back. Why wasn't Ben agreeing?

Finally Ben sighed and met his gaze. "You're right. And that's what Dani said too. I know it's true."

Léo closed his eyes. "But you're going anyway." He let go of Ben's hands and ran his fingers through his hair, a nervous habit his nanny had broken him of when he was a child.

"I'm going anyway," Ben confirmed. "I honestly don't want to, and I'm positive I'll be back. But if I don't, I'm always going to worry. This is going to nag at me, and eventually it'll cause problems between us. I'd rather take a few months now to set my mind at rest. Please try to understand."

Léo sighed. "When are you going?" Ben's wince confirmed his worst fears. "No. You cannot just announce this and leave. I get tonight. If you're going to leave me for four months, I get you tonight."

Ben hesitated, then nodded. "Okay. We can have tonight." He sat back down beside Léo, then climbed into his lap and leaned his head against Léo's. "I love you," he whispered. "I love you more than I could have imagined. I remember when I first saw you, and it's like a scene in a movie. In my head, music plays and everything goes out of focus except you."

Léo wanted to chuckle, to tease Ben, but all he could think was that in a few short hours Ben would be leaving, his bunny, gone, and he'd be alone in this apartment that was stupidly big for a single man. He would have nobody to eat breakfast with, nobody to check in with before making plans. Nobody would come and knock on the door while he was working and offer him coffee, and nobody would cringe and pretend to hide it when he used valet parking.

He kissed Ben. He yanked at his shirt, desperate to feel the warm skin beneath, to be in control for just a little while longer. Ben's hands were on Léo's trousers, just as desperate, and soon they were naked, kissing, rubbing against each other, working themselves into a frenzy.

"Bedroom," Léo panted, but Ben shook his head.

"No, here."

"We don't have supplies," Léo argued, then moaned as Ben grabbed his dick and *squeezed*. "Do that again," he gasped. Ben obliged, then let go. He bent over the arm of the couch, nearly giving Léo a heart attack with the view, and then a moment later he was back, wriggling against Léo's lap, a condom in one hand and a small bottle of lube in the other.

"I never put them away after that time—" he began, but Léo fused their mouths together, not *caring*. The only thing that mattered was Ben.

Ben, who was opening the lube, slicking his fingers, prepping himself, right there in Léo's lap. He gave Léo the condom, and Léo scrambled to get it on. In no time, Ben was lowering himself onto Léo's dick, and then they were joined, and Léo's chest ached, because tomorrow, he wouldn't have this anymore. His bunny would be *gone*. He forced the thought away, focusing instead on Ben's hips under his hands, his neck and collarbone under Léo's mouth, the tight grip of him around Léo's cock, the noises he made as Léo made sure to hit his prostate. He knew Ben could come from this alone, but this time, their last time together for months, he wanted to show Ben who was in charge.

He grabbed Ben's dick where it was pressed between them, leaking precum against Léo's stomach, and stroked. Ben moaned.

Léo squeezed.

Ben gasped, his rhythm faltering, and Léo let go.

"Noooooo," Ben implored.

"Keep moving," Léo gritted out, and as Ben hastened to comply, he slid his hand over his bunny's cock again, feathering over the sensitive head, down the shaft, trailing his fingers along the soft skin of Ben's balls, drawn up so tight. He was nearly there, so Léo tickled delicately, trying to ignore the tight, heavy feeling in his own balls, Ben's desperate "Ungh!" music to his ears.

His questing fingers stroked up Ben's crack, to where

he could feel himself sliding in and out of Ben's gorgeous arse—

"Arrrgh!" Ben cried, and his chute constricted around Léo for long seconds, releasing then tightening again—and again. Léo lost control, coming so hard his vision blurred, and when his brain came back online, Ben was draped over him, face buried in Léo's neck, panting.

Léo turned his head and kissed Ben's hair.

"I love you," he whispered. "Please come back to me."

Chapter Thirteen

Ben sat outdoors at a café in Piazza San Marco and gazed at the basilica. With the deepening twilight, the lights were coming on, and the building had the same glow as so many of the historic structures he'd seen in Europe. The weather was colder than he'd expected when he'd been planning the trip—after all, it was November, not July as he'd originally intended—and with many fewer tourists, but Venice was still as incredible as he'd imagined. Lucien had been right—he liked it best of all the places he'd seen in Italy.

Lucien had, unfortunately, also been right that Venice was best visited in company. Everywhere Ben looked, he saw people in groups. Couples. Even those who seemed to be alone were usually just waiting for others to join them. In the four days he'd already been in Venice, he could count on one hand the number of people he'd seen who had actually been on their own—and he'd have fingers leftover.

Ben missed Léo desperately. They'd spoken every day since he'd left Monaco a little under four weeks ago, texting often and actually talking or FaceTiming at least once a day. On several occasions, Léo had been out with Malik or Lucien when Ben called, or Ben had been doing something suitably touristy when Léo called, and missing out on his Léo time had caused an actual physical ache in his chest.

Ben had taken his time traveling through Italy, really immersing himself in the country. It was beautiful. He'd seen all the places he'd read about, eaten what had felt like his own weight in food at every meal, and learned so much about the culture. Italy was an amazing country. It was everything he'd dreamed.

But it wasn't Monaco.

It wasn't a city-state built on a hill where around every corner there was a view of the ocean. Every time he went to a market, or bought cheap T-shirts from a street hawker, he was reminded of the place where such things were anathema. The glory of ancient cities and the compelling juxtaposition of historic structures beside modern buildings paled beside the memory of casual glamour and elegance. Even the displays of wealth, far more than he was used to seeing in Australia—this was Europe, after all —seemed not as natural.

He was being silly, of course. It was all in his head— well, mostly—but that didn't make it any less difficult to handle. Not for the first time, he regretted his decision to take the same amount of time he'd spent in Monaco for his travels. It hadn't even been a month, and already he wanted to go home to Léo.

In his hand, his phone trilled, and Ben's mood lifted. He'd been expecting Léo to call, and here he was, right on time.

"Hello?" he said eagerly.

"Hello, Bunny," Léo said, and Ben laughed. Léo had

explained the whole "bunny" thing during a marathon call several weeks back, and although it had been a little weird at first, the affection in Léo's voice when he said it ensured that Ben had grown to love the endearment.

"Hey. How was the drive?" he asked. Léo had been in Paris for the past four days, meeting his brand-new nephew and doing his duty by his family. He'd flown up, but then decided to drive back, stopping overnight to visit with a friend in Lyon.

He'd bought a new car for the drive. Ben had winced when he'd heard, and Léo, laughing, had assured him that it was not an extravagant car. Ben had looked it up after the call and was now completely certain that he and Léo had different definitions of "extravagant."

"It was good to drive," Léo said. "It's been a long time since I've driven farther than Nice. How is Venice this evening?"

"Magical," Ben said, looking around the piazza again. And it *was*. Somehow, in the past two minutes it had transformed from merely incredible to beyond description.

He tried not to dwell on why that might be.

"I splurged and took a water taxi down the Grand Canal to St. Mark's at twilight, like Malik suggested. Honestly, does he know every possible romantic place and activity in the world? He's done that before with a woman, hasn't he?"

"Women," Léo said, laughing. "We spent a month in Venice the summer we were twenty, and Malik had a water taxi on retainer for the same time every night. Even now, if you mention his name to the taxi operators there, they smirk."

Ben giggled and made a mental note to try that.

"Tell me what else you did today," Léo prompted, and Ben did. Then he asked about Léo's day, most of which

had been spent in his car, and heard about Malik's relief
that Léo was back and could save him from the tourist
who'd fallen in love with him.

"*What?*" Ben demanded, not sure whether he should
laugh and kind of wanting to. "How did a tourist fall in
love with him in four days, and how are you supposed to
save him?"

"I have no idea, to both those questions," Léo
answered. "With Malik, sometimes it's better not to ask.
He will be here soon, and I'm sure I will hear all about it
then."

"He's coming over? Are you guys going out?" Ben
asked wistfully.

"Not tonight. Lucien's coming—his plane should land
soon—and we are supposed to review some papers for one
of his mother's charities. Malik decided he didn't want to
be left out and promised to bring dinner if we let him
come."

"Why didn't you look at the papers while you were in
Paris?" The sudden sharp longing was hard to ignore.

"I was going to," Léo admitted, "but then I didn't want
to stay in Paris that long, and Lucien wanted to get out of
Paris for a couple of days, so… it seemed opportune."

"Yeah." A thought struck. "Malik's bringing dinner?
He's not cooking it, surely?"

Léo's laughter warmed him from the inside out—
which was good, because it was getting damn cold now,
especially with the wind picking up.

"No, he's not cooking it," Léo assured him. "And if he
ever does offer to cook for you, say no. He can barely mix
a drink. He'll have one of his favorite restaurants cater the
meal."

That made much more sense. Ben hadn't been able to
imagine Malik ordering a cheap, greasy takeaway—or Léo

and Lucien eating it, for that matter, even if there had been somewhere nearby that did casual takeaway. Malik and Léo had spoken fondly of their time at Oxford, eating pub food and generally living the student life, but that was years ago, and Ben had never seen them eat less than the best.

In the background, he heard the sound of Léo's doorbell, and his stomach sank.

"I have to go," Léo said, regret clear in his voice.

"I know," Ben replied. "I'll talk to you tomorrow?" He winced at how needy he sounded.

"Of course. I love you."

Ben smiled, his heart breaking. "I love you too."

They ended the call, and for a moment he stared at the phone in his hand. Would it be completely selfish if he…?

Yes, it would be, he decided. Then he did it anyway.

"'Lo? Ben?" Dani croaked. "Are you okay?" Remorse swamped him, but not enough to make him hang up.

"I'm fine. I'm sorry to wake you." He glanced at his watch and cringed. She needed to get up for work in just a few hours.

"What's wrong?" she asked, sounding slightly more alert. He heard rustling, presumably her sheets as she sat up in bed. Dani always propped herself against the headboard when she spoke on the phone in bed.

"Nothing's wrong, really." He sighed. "I guess I'm just lonely. I was talking to Léo, and he had to go because Malik and Lucien were coming over, and… I really wished I was there."

"He didn't make you feel like he was too busy for you, did he?" Dani demanded, the fierce lioness coming to the fore.

"No, nothing like that." Ben smiled. "If I'd asked him

to, he probably would have kept me on speaker phone so I could spend the evening with them."

"So you're not worried that his feelings are fading?" There was an edge of sarcasm to her voice.

Ben chuckled. "No way. He loves me." He was sure of that now. This past month had concreted it in his mind.

"And you love him?"

"Of course." He really shouldn't have woken her. She was obviously so tired she couldn't process properly.

"Then why the fuck are you alone in Venice, missing him, wishing you were there, and waking me up at... Christ, three o'clock in the morning to whine about it?" She sounded pissed off, and thinking about it, he could see why.

He started to laugh. A real, hearty, full-blown laugh that made the few other patrons willing to risk the cold and sit outside turn to look.

"I'm an idiot, aren't I, Dani?" he asked.

"Yes. You're a complete moron. What are you doing right now?"

Ben looked around. "I'm sitting in St. Mark's Square, freezing my arse off while I drink incredibly overpriced coffee with liqueur in it and stare at the basilica."

"Right. Well, I suggest you pay for that very expensive coffee, go back to your hotel, and pack. Get online and book a flight for tomorrow morning that will get you back to where you really want to be. Sort things out with Léo, and when you guys are all settled into domestic bliss, you can see the other places on your list *together*. Sound good?"

"Sounds great," Ben affirmed. "You always did make the best plans. Will you come and spend Christmas with us? It might snow." He thought about it. "Well, probably not in Monaco, but we can go someplace where it will."

"Probably not, Ben," she said quietly, and he frowned.

"I can't tempt you with a white Christmas?" he teased, wondering what was wrong. She chuckled a little.

"I don't want to leave right now, Benji. Gran's not doing well."

Ben winced. He was such an arse. "I'm sorry, Dani. Why didn't you say anything? Do you want me to come back? I can look after her for you. And don't call me Benji," he tacked on.

"No, honey. Thanks for offering, but I would rather poke out my own eyes than keep you away from Léo for even a second longer than necessary. We've got things handled here."

"Are you sure?" Ben wished he could make this easier for Dani. He'd had to watch many times as people said goodbye to loved ones, and nothing about it was good.

"I'm sure. Now, I'm going to go back to sleep, and you need to get moving if you're going back to Monaco tomorrow."

"True. Okay. I'm sorry I had to wake you, but not sorry we talked. I'll call you when I'm back at Léo's. Good night, Dani."

"Night, Benji." She hung up before he could tell her not to call him Benji. He signaled to the waiter that he wanted his bill, and then while he waited he googled possible flights to Monaco. It wasn't encouraging. There weren't many direct from Venice, so he'd have to transit via somewhere else.

The waiter brought a discreet leather folder, and Ben hurried to pull out his wallet and pay. Once he'd put far too much money down, he stood up so sharply that he knocked over his chair, and when he bent over to right it, he bashed his forehead on the table.

"Fuck!" Rubbing his head, he straightened, deciding to just leave the chair, and waved off the concerned waiter.

Shivering slightly, he began walking back toward his hotel… and then stopped. The hotel wasn't too far, sure, and water taxis were horrifically expensive, but it was cold. He had stuff to do. And he had the money. Maybe he had to get used to using it.

Determined, he turned and went to the taxi rank. Within ten minutes, he was back at the berth nearest his hotel—right in front, actually—and as he handed over the necessary euros, he realized the little niggle of guilt for not walking was easier to ignore than he'd thought. Maybe he would never be able to spend money as casually as Léo, but sometimes, on special occasions, he could splash out a bit. Like he had on his hotels this trip. The place he was staying was the height of luxury, and that meant it wasn't cheap.

He was halfway across the hotel lobby before that thought sank in. He looked around. It really was a luxurious hotel. That meant staff who were ready and waiting to assist guests. And being not-cheap—really fucking not-cheap, to be honest—meant the staff were used to catering to people who had money and weren't afraid to spend it.

He turned around and went over to the concierge desk. The man there smiled at him. Ben smiled back.

"I need to get to Monaco as fast as possible."

Chapter Fourteen

Two hours later, Ben climbed out of the helicopter that had whisked him from Venice to Monaco, clutching his carry-on bag. The pilot jumped down and passed his suitcase to the driver of the car waiting to take him to Léo's apartment. Ben followed the driver numbly.

He wasn't sure if he ever wanted to get into a helicopter again. Yes, it had been quicker than a plane, and definitely more convenient. But not more comfortable. And oh my God, the price had been horrifying.

He slid into the luxury sedan and admitted to himself that sometimes it was worth paying a little more for comfort. If he'd been in any other place, he'd probably have tried to get a train or something, and this car shit on any train he'd ever been on.

As the car wound through increasingly familiar streets, anxiety kicked in. Should he have called and told Léo he was coming? Really, why hadn't he? He knew Léo would be glad to see him. He probably even had a friend who could have given him a lift.

Worrying won't help anything. You're nearly there. It was all going to be okay. He loved Léo. Léo loved him. Léo would be thrilled to see him. They would make love and snuggle and stay up all night talking.

Well, maybe not the last. But they would talk. There was no way Ben could go on without working. It would drive him insane. He had his long-stay visa, so he'd jump through whatever hoops necessary to gain work privileges, and then he'd look into temp jobs. Maybe there were rich old people who only needed short-term nurses while they were visiting Monaco? Or Léo probably knew someone who could help him. Working full-time would eat into the time he could spend with Léo, and really, he didn't need to. They both had money. Why take a job someone else really needed? Relief and temp work was fine with him.

He and Léo could travel too. Ben wanted to spend more time in Venice, and he hadn't gotten to Switzerland, Austria, Germany, and the rest yet, and he wouldn't mind going back to the UK. Hadn't Malik said a while back that he and Léo usually spent a few weeks skiing in Switzerland every year?

Ben had been skiing once. It had been a pretty disastrous experience, but he had fond memories of sitting in front of the fire at the lodge with a hot, doctored drink, gossiping with Dani. He could do that while Léo skied.

And maybe he could get involved with some charity work. It would be nice to give something back, now that he really could.

Of course, it all depended on whether Léo was pleased to see him or not.

Ben shook his head firmly as they pulled up in front of Léo's building. He was being silly. He tipped the driver, waited patiently while the man unloaded his suitcase, even though he could have done it himself, and then squared his shoulders as he looked at the glass doors in front of him. The doorman looked back. Ben didn't recognize him, and another bout of nerves jabbed sharply at his stomach.

This is stupid. The longer you stand out here like a moron, the longer you're away from Léo.

He sucked in a deep breath and walked toward the door. The doorman snapped to attention and opened it for him. Ben smiled at him and walked through, dragging his suitcase behind him.

Inside, he noted with some relief that he knew the man at the security desk, who was smiling at him with faint surprise.

"Monsieur Adams, welcome back," the man—Ben was pretty sure his name was Marc—said politely. "May I take your bag?"

"That's okay, I've got it," Ben said, as breezily as he could manage considering that his throat felt tight. "I'm just going to head straight up."

"Bien sûr, monsieur."

The lift was waiting, and Ben stepped inside and hit the button for Léo's floor. As usual, the ride was smooth, silent, and fast. It seemed only seconds later that he was standing in front of Léo's door.

And the nerves disappeared.

Grinning broadly, he knocked. He actually still had a key, but in the rush of packing he'd forgotten to find it, and it was somewhere in his luggage.

The door opened, and Ben found himself face-to-face with Malik, whose eyes got very wide. Then a beautiful smile spread across his face. He glanced over his shoulder, then stepped out into the hall and pulled the door nearly all the way closed.

"I'd ask if he knew you were coming, but if he did he'd be in a better mood." Malik looked him up and down, and then reached out and yanked him into a rough hug. "It's good to see you. Is this just a visit, or—"

"I'm home." The words tasted wonderful in his mouth.

Malik grinned again. "It's good to have you home. Come on, I want to see his face." He pushed the door open and ushered Ben in, grabbing his suitcase for him.

As he closed the door, Léo called something in French. It was a little fast for Ben's still-learning ear, but the gist seemed to be "Who was at the door?"

Malik called back, something about a package—a delivery, maybe?—and gestured for Ben to precede him.

Ben walked into the living room just as Léo was headed toward the door, muttering about not ordering anything. They both froze. On the couch, Lucien gave a delighted cry and sprang to his feet.

Ben met Léo's gaze and swallowed hard. He'd missed him so much. "Hey," he said. Léo's dark eyes skimmed over him.

"You're in Venice," he said.

Ben shook his head. "I was. But I wanted to be here, so…." He spread his hands. "I'm here."

Léo's jaw tightened. "For how long?"

Suddenly, Ben realized how much he'd hurt Léo with his insistence that he needed to test their feelings for each other, with this enforced separation.

I'm such a dick.

"Forever," he said. "I'm sorry. I shouldn't have gone. But I'm back now, and I'm never leaving you again. I love you."

In three long strides, Léo closed the space between them, snatching Ben into his arms and kissing him so hard Ben was sure his lips went numb.

He didn't care.

He was dimly aware of Malik and Lucien cheering in the background, but his focus was on the feel of Léo under his hands, his smell, his taste. Something inside him clicked into place. He hadn't even noticed how stressed he'd been until this moment when, finally safe in Léo's arms, everything in him relaxed.

When they finally pulled back for air, Léo was smiling, and Ben grinned delightedly in response.

"Champagne!" Lucien announced, shoving two glasses toward them. Ben turned and saw Malik pouring more of the pale gold liquid. Because of course Léo had had a bottle of his favorite—and now Ben's favorite—champagne chilling. He took the glasses and handed one to Léo. Within moments, they all had a glass in hand.

"I would toast," Malik said, "but I'd rather get on with the celebration."

Ben laughed, his free hand clasped snugly in Léo's.

"By all means," Léo agreed, "drink your champagne and go so we can get on with the celebration."

Heat flared in Ben's cheeks as Malik and Lucien hooted, and he closed his eyes. A moment later, lips brushed his, and he lifted his lids to look into Léo's beautiful dark eyes. Amusement shone there, but also love, and Ben forgot his embarrassment.

"Welcome home, Bunny."

I hope you enjoyed *Charming Him*! Next up is *Offside Rules,* where Lucien meets his match in retired soccer player, Simon.

To talk spoilers and hear what's next, join the chat in my
Facebook group, RoMMance with Becca & Louisa
Or you can subscribe to my newsletter to get all updates
and access to bonus scenes: https://bit.ly/LouisaMBonus.

Interested in exclusive bonus scenes, serials, early chapters,
and artwork? Check out my Patreon: https://www.
patreon.com/louisamasters

Also by Louisa Masters

Saddles & Suits
Alistair's Extraordinaries
Grave Situation
Elemental Men: The Complete Series

Style Me
Rebrand
Couture

Elf Magic
Wooing the Wiccan
Enticing the Elf

The Collective
Higher Demon
Demon Hunter

Demons-In-Law
Asher
Micah
Zachary

Franklin U
Mr. Romance
The Holigay Hookup *related novella
Batting Style

Ghostly Guardians

Spirited Situation

Vortex Conundrum

Conduit Crisis

Gateway Catastrophe

Here Be Dragons

Dragon Ever After

The Professor's Dragon

The Dragon Experiment

Conspiracy of Dragons

Hidden Species

Demons Do It Better

One Bite With A Vampire

Hijinks With A Hellhound

Sorcerers Always Satisfy

Hidden Species Box Set

Met His Match

Charming Him

Offside Rules

A Christmas Chance (novella)

Between the Covers (M/F)

Joy Universe

I've Got This

Follow My Lead

In Your Hands

Take Us There

Novellas

Fake It 'Til You Make It (permafree)

One Golden Night

O Hell, All Ye Shoppers

Out of the Office

After the Blaze

Blokes Down Under Novella Collection

About the Author

Louisa Masters started reading romance much earlier than her mother thought she should. As an adult, she feeds her addiction in every spare second. She spent years trying to build a "sensible" career, working in bookstores, recruitment, resource management, administration, and as a travel agent before finally conceding defeat and devoting herself to the world of romance novels.

Louisa has a long list of places first discovered in books that she wants to visit, and every so often she overcomes her loathing of jet lag and takes a trip that charges her imagination. She lives in Melbourne, Australia, where she whines about the weather for most of the year while secretly admitting she'll probably never move.

http://www.louisamasters.com